D0007200

THE GREAT GOD PAN

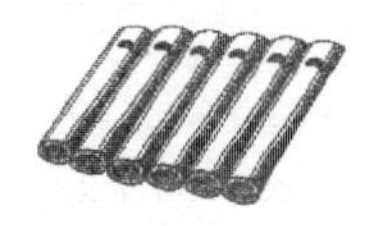

Other Books by Donna Jo Napoli

For Young Adults

Changing Tunes
The Bravest Thing
Jimmy, the Pickpocket of the Palace
The Prince of the Pond: Otherwise Known as De Fawg Pin
Shark Shock
Soccer Shock
Shelley Shock
On Guard
When the Water Closes Over My Head
The Magic Circle
Zel
Song of the Magdalene
Trouble on the Tracks
For the Love of Venice
Stones in Water
Sirena
Crazy Jack
Spinners *(with Richard Tchen)*
Three Days
Beast
Daughter of Venice

For Younger Readers

The Hero of Barletta
Albert
Rocky the Cat Who Barks *(with Marie Kane)*
How Hungry Are You? *(with Richard Tchen)*
Flamingo Dream
Angelwings (a series of sixteen books)

the great god PAN

donna jo napoli

WENDY LAMB BOOKS

Published by
Wendy Lamb Books
an imprint of
Random House Children's Books
a division of Random House, Inc.
New York

Visit us on the Web! www.randomhouse.com/teens
Educators and librarians, for a variety of teaching tools, visit us at
www.randomhouse.com/teachers

Library of Congress Cataloging-in-Publication Data
Napoli, Donna Jo.
The great god Pan / Donna Jo Napoli.
p. cm.
Summary: A retelling of the Greek myths about Pan, both goat and god, whose reed flute frolicking leads him to a meeting with Iphigenia, a human raised as the daughter of King Agamemnon and Queen Clytemnestra.
ISBN 0-385-32777-3 (trade) — ISBN 0-385-90120-8 (GLB)
1. Pan (Greek deity)—Juvenile fiction. [1. Pan (Greek deity)—Fiction.
2. Mythology, Greek—Fiction.] I. Title.
PZ7.N15 Gr 2003
[Fic]—dc21 2002013139

The text of this book is set in 11-point Galliard.
Book design by Trish Parcell Watts
Printed in the United States of America
May 2003
10 9 8 7 6 5 4 3 2 1
BVG

For Helen Plotkin,

with admiration

and gratitude

and love

Acknowledgments

My usual vast thanks go to Barry and Nick and Eva and Robert, for nurturing me through every phase. For help on so many things in so many ways, I thank Julie Nishimura-Jensen, Jodi Kreitzman, Rosaria Munson, Lindsey Newbold, Rio Perzan, Helen Plotkin, Eric Raimy, Alison Root, Gil Rose, Richard Tchen, William Turpin, Jennifer Wingertzahn, and Chandra Yesiltas. Thanks also go to Lynn Oberfield's ninth-grade language arts class at Strath Haven High School in spring 2000.
And, most of all, thanks to Wendy Lamb.

genealogy of the gods in this tale

(Mortals are in *italics*)

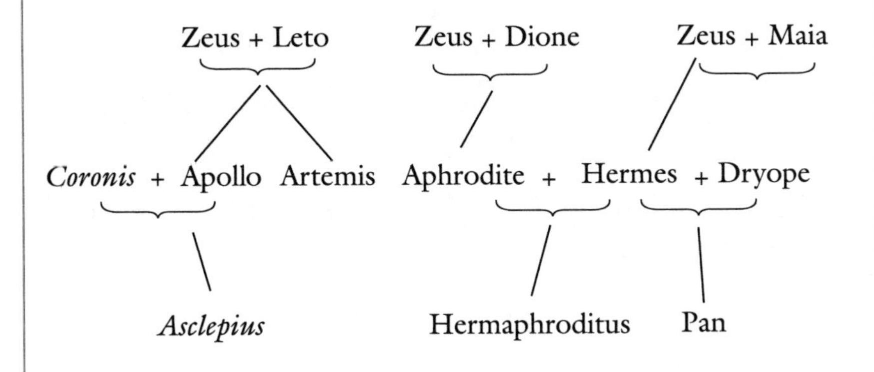

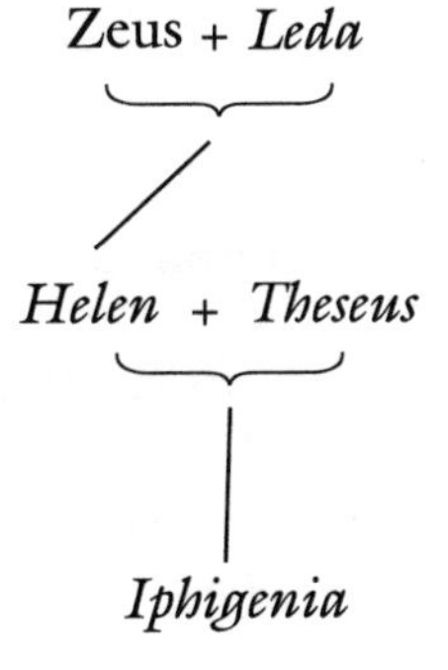

cast of characters

Aphrodite: Olympian goddess of love and beauty

Apollo: Olympian god of the arts, archery, and divination; twin of Artemis

Artemis: Olympian goddess of the hunt; protector of maidens; twin of Apollo

Asclepius: mortal; famous surgeon; child of Apollo and the mortal Coronis

Coronis: mortal; mother of Asclepius

Dione: goddess, perhaps originally from mythology of Asia Minor; mother of Aphrodite by Zeus

Dryope: nymph; mother of Pan by Hermes

Helen: mortal; said to be the most beautiful woman in the world; child of the mortal Leda by Zeus; Queen of Sparta

Hera: Olympian goddess of marriage; wife of Zeus

Hermaphroditus: child of Aphrodite and Hermes; had both male and female characteristics

Hermes: Olympian god of merchants and trickery; protector of travelers; herald of the gods; father of Pan

Iphigenia: mortal; daughter of Helen and the mortal Theseus; raised as the daughter of King Agamemnon and Queen Clytemnestra

Leda: mortal; mother of Helen by Zeus

Leto: Titan goddess; mother of the twins Apollo and Artemis by Zeus

Maia: daughter of the Titan Atlas; mother of Hermes by Zeus

Pan: Ah, for this, dear soul, read on.

Theseus: mortal of royal descent; father of Iphigenia

Zeus: Olympian god of the sky; ruler of Olympus; husband of Hera; prolific father

part one

FATEFUL MEETINGS

chapter one

FATHER

"Pan!" booms the voice I know so well. "Come with me to Olympus."

"Father!" I jump up and trot to him. We hug. "What sudden pleasure."

Father's face glows. "Pleasure? Yes. But for now we have to hurry. The gods are fighting on Olympus, and—"

"The same old thing." I cut him off. "Squabbles among the gods bore me."

"This squabble appears to be important. Hera's furious at Zeus."

"Hera's always furious at Zeus," I say. "He's the most roving husband ever and she's the most nagging wife ever."

"This is different."

"What harm can one squabble make?"

"There's been a prophecy of war in a year or two."

Father rubs the back of his neck. Then he laughs. "But in the long term, none of it is of any consequence. People die and we gods go on forever, regardless."

"So forget Olympus," I say. "Explore the meadow. The air sings with spring."

We walk side by side, though it's all I can do to keep from prancing in excitement; visits from Father are always fun. He is Hermes, the god of trickery, after all—he loves a good joke.

There's another hour or two of light left before night; we can share the best time of day. I let loose and run in a circle around him, climb every boulder we pass, jump and skip.

After a while, Father stops to adjust his winged slippers. He doesn't say anything, but I can see his annoyance. Nature doesn't hold his attention the way it holds mine. And he'd rather fly wherever he goes.

But I have hooves that take off at a walk, a trot, a run, before I can even think to stop them. I have to make this walk exciting for Father if I'm going to keep him with me.

A man on horseback cuts through the trees beyond the meadow. What luck. I lift my eyebrows at Father.

"Ah, could be good sport," he says, and we race after the horseman.

The man jumps off and joins a group of three other men sitting in a circle. We watch from behind a tree.

"The caravan will be here within the hour," says the horseman.

"How many guards?" asks one man.

"Two," says the horseman.

"The fools," says another man.

"Are you sure there's enough there to make it worth the danger?" asks the third.

"It's carrying the Queen of Argos' jewels, you idiot."

Father and I back away till we're out of earshot.

"Outlaws deserve tricks," says Father with a grin.

I'm already way ahead of him. "Follow me." I race through the trees and across the meadow, where I see the familiar row of woven wicker baskets attached to the fence, each holding a hive—a bee farm.

Aha! A bee zips past my nose. She's a scout. Bees have swarmed and left their hive; the workers congregate on a branch with their queen. I inspect the old hives in the baskets. We're lucky: Another is just about ready to swarm. I free the basket from the fence and hold it out toward Father.

He puts his hands up. "You're the god of beekeeping, Pan, not me. Besides, I've got sensitive skin and you're a hairy brute." He laughs.

From the waist down I'm goat. But above the waist the only hints of goat are my ears and horns and the fur on my cheeks. My torso skin is just like his. But there's no point arguing—he's afraid of the bees and I'm not.

The hive inside the basket buzzes loudly, ready to sting. I run as fast as I can toward the road, where a carriage rattles along. Father flies ahead of me. I hear women screaming, but by the time I reach the caravan, Father has explained the situation and calmed everyone down. The sight of me starts them screaming all over again. Typical human dunces.

The Queen of Argos isn't in this caravan—she follows tomorrow.

The servants open the jewelry box and stuff the queen's necklaces and armbands and other baubles here and there about their persons. When the box is empty, I drop in the hive basket and close the box so fast, I escape without a sting.

The servants get back into the caravan with the box and continue on their way. Father and I follow, covered by the trees that flank the road.

The outlaws burst into view on horses.

"Aiii!" the servants howl. "Thieves!" They hand over the box. I wish we could hear what everyone's saying—we're missing half the fun.

The outlaws gallop off into the trees as the caravan leaves. Father flies after the outlaws and I race behind. We find them hunched over, opening the jewelry box.

Perfect. The hive swarms. Bees in the outlaws' hair and noses and mouths. Clouds of bees chase the men to their horses, horses that bolted at the first buzz. Horses and men mix helter-skelter, shouting and neighing, as Father and I fall on each other, laughing. We leap out at them, and the shouts turn to screams. Wonderful chaos.

"Panic," says Father proudly. "Pan causes panic."

"Come home with me, Father." I take him by the hand and pull him along. "I'll make you all your favorite foods. Come."

And he does. Father has so many children, yet I'm the one he visits most often. I never knew my mother, but I know my father very well. We eat and drink late into the night; then I prepare a bed of the densest, most fragrant fir needles in the deepest part of the cave and convince Father to spend the night.

The sound of his sleeping breath makes me smile. We got through the whole evening without an argument about how I live. He didn't even criticize the slovenly condition of my cave.

I lie awake listening to the mingling of our breaths, and look forward to sweet dreams.

chapter two

SCORPIONS

"You are unwashed, hairy, noisy, inconstant, and smelly."

I wake and blink, clearing my eyes to the morning's gift of a maenad leaning into my cave. She gives a little yank to a tuft of my cheek fur and grins down at me. For all the world, I swear that the woman is as beautiful as Aphrodite, despite her uncombed hair and wild eyes, or, rather, because of them. Others may call maenads maddened women, but I find their free ways all the more delicious. "Sweet thing," I whisper with a grin that matches hers, "am I really that attractive?" I put a finger to my lips. Father is still asleep.

"Half goat, half man. Perfect Pan." She shimmies. "You're awake, shaggy fellow, so get up. Come play." She runs her toes along my ribs.

I grab her foot and nibble.

She laughs. "Unfair. Just because you have no toes to torment." She leans over and raps her knuckles on my right hoof. Then she pulls me to a stand. "My sisters are out of sight already. We have to hurry to catch up. Really."

I stretch my arm around the maenad's waist and dance with her, flailing and flopping. A yellow cloud of pollen rises from our stomping. The flowers let out gasps of gratitude. We go faster, always laughing. She shrieks as we tumble down the grassy slope and land near a small pond.

A dragonfly hovers over us. His segmented tail twitches, his wings shimmer. The maenad smiles at him, then untangles her hair from my horns. "Clumsy Pan." She licks my nose. "And salty. Have you every virtue?"

"He's my son, isn't he?" Father appears beside us.

The maenad scrambles to her feet. "Great god Hermes," she says, her eyes lowered.

I stand. "Good morning, Father. I hope you slept well."

"I leave you to the pleasure of each other's company."

But the maenad already runs in the direction of her sisters. "Farewell, great Hermes," she calls. "Until the next time, Pan." Her giggle fades in the distance.

Father watches her enter the wood and disappear. "Could a mere maenad bring much pleasure?"

Mere? The maenads are my best friends. They are dear. I'm glad this one didn't hear Father—she might have winced. But I don't challenge him. After all, I can tell from the tone of his voice, the tap of his foot, that he's considering a frolic. As usual. "They make me laugh," I say.

"Are they as much fun as ordinary humans?"

Ordinary humans are rude to me, like those stupid servants in the caravan yesterday. At least until they find out I'm a god. I avoid them. The maenads, on the other hand, are extraordinary humans. They've abandoned town life, leaving behind civilization's rules to follow their natural impulses, many of which suit me perfectly. "I wouldn't know."

"Hmmm. Maenads welcome anyone in their drunken frenzies, even satyrs." He winks. "My son can do better."

Satyrs are bestial and crude—half goat, half human. Ignorant souls confuse me with them, but the maenads know I'm no satyr. They must. Don't they? "The maenads welcome me, Father. They welcome Pan."

"Well, at least they're mortal," says Father. "So if you get mixed up with one and things go wrong, you don't have to put up with her for long."

"Mixed up?"

"You know what I mean, Pan. You're foolish enough to let yourself feel genuine affection, despite the curse."

The curse. I stamp a hoof in annoyance at that stupid curse. And I think the idea stinks that maenads are fine to dally with because they die. My father can be such a louse. I yank at a dandelion puff. "Flowers are mortal." I blow the seeds in his face. "And immortal. In their own way."

"Spoken like the god of nature that you are." Father

laughs agreeably. "Okay, stick to those lovelies. Better them than immortal nymphs."

Nymphs, who are the most beautiful of creatures, have always found me ugly and disgusting. But the maenads enjoy me just as I am. That's why I prefer them—not because they're mortal. This line of talk gets ever more irritating.

"Are you ready to come to Olympus?" Father brushes the dandelion seeds away. "And maybe stay this time. Live with the gods and enjoy your true home again."

I knew this was coming. "I told you yesterday, go without me."

"Calm down, there's no cause for anger." Father flicks his fingers on the back of my pointed ear. "Little god, little goat."

His finger-flicks tickle. He does this whenever I'm mad at him, and it always works; I can't help but laugh. My whole life, Father and I have laughed together.

"You'll have fun," he says. "Everyone on Olympus misses you. You're their favorite."

"But I hate these meetings. Don't make me come."

"All right," says Father. "For this time. I'll tell everyone you needed to go scattering seeds." He winks; then he hugs me and disappears. Gone. Just like that.

I wander.

The day started so full—two visitors. Now it seems empty.

But what a foolish thought. The morning is noisy with life making new life. A woodpecker bangs rhythmically, calling for a mate so late in the season. He's right: On a spring day anything is possible.

I walk faster. This is my realm—the meadows and forests and beasts and all nature—even human nature.

Heaps of stones stretch out ahead. I let out a whoop and leap from pinnacle to pinnacle. I leap and leap and—Ahiiii! Fiery pain shoots up the middle of my left hoof. I grab it with both hands and hop. A half-mashed scorpion writhes where I stepped.

"Gods are immortal!" I scream. "You can't kill me." But you can paralyze me, I'm thinking, you can make me miserable. I pick up a stone and pound the scorpion till the pieces scatter, all the while balancing on one hoof.

My head is hot with fear. Have I been poisoned? But breath comes easy. No wheezing. My vision is clear. My mouth is dry. Good signs, the surgeon Asclepius would say. I examine the underside of my left hoof. The soft fleshy center quickly swells, but the pain already subsides.

I lower my face to the remnants of the scorpion. "You're dead for eternity, while I'll hobble for a day at most." That's what happens when a mortal creature takes on a god.

But now the pieces of the creature look pathetic. This is a morning of dragonflies and scorpions—small life, which larger forms depend upon in ways they cannot guess. And what else could the scorpion do but sting? I stepped on it.

I tap the pieces with my fingertips, drawing them together. Unlucky soul.

Two huge scorpions bask in the sun on the rock just ahead. One is male, the other female.

I rub my hands in delight. "May your spirit watch," I whisper to the dead scorpion.

I close my eyes, my ears, my limbs. I shrink inward—my chest squeezes to almost nothing. My outsides crackle as I implode.

I am scorpion.

With both pincers raised, I walk across rock face toward the male. He jumps to attention and raises his own pincers. He seemed tiny a moment ago and now he could rip a pincer off me. Or a leg. I'd be deformed forever.

I stop.

I should transform back to my true self. Consoling the spirit of the scorpion isn't worth the risk.

I did kill him, though, and all I need now is a few minutes to set things right. A few minutes.

And luck.

My innards shake.

I back up.

The male runs at me, stops, and waves those pincers. Is the female blind, that she takes no notice?

I tremble and back up more, so scared that I can barely hold this form.

The female stirs at last. She lifts her thin tail, and the sharp curving stinger drops venom from the tip. Delicate.

Arousing. I know everything this female wants. I know everything this male wants.

This is why I change shapes. This is how I know nature better than anyone else.

I'm caught between the scorpions, both of whom would kill me in their own way. My fear grows until I race to the edge of the rock and throw myself off, not an instant too soon: I transform in midair.

And crash into a boulder. I put my hands to the base of my horns. Oh, my poor head.

I limp back to the scorpions to see that they dance across the rock, tails intertwined over their heads, her pincers trapped in his.

After mating, he skitters away, but she catches his tail, flips him, and they fight. He's faster; she's larger. I back away as the female eats the male. It seems a mistake of nature that mating should be so dangerous.

My fingertips sweep together the pieces of the scorpion I crushed. "See? The eggs that will hatch inside the female are my gift to you. A replacement, of sorts. Now we're even."

Except that my head throbs where I smashed it and my hoof hurts a little still. I look around, fearful. But why? There's no reason I should feel this way.

chapter three

NYMPHS

Gnats come from nowhere and swarm around my sticky head as I walk. I swat them away and trot, flicking my ears.

The way Father flicked them when he called me little goat.

I am half goat, half god because of Father. Hybrid.

The story of my curse began when Father saw his half sister, Aphrodite, bathing in the River Achelous in all her splendid beauty and sent an eagle to steal her sandal. He wouldn't give it back until she agreed to lie with him. This much is not unusual: The Olympian gods have the habit of taking pleasure whether it's offered or not. Even from a sister.

Aphrodite had a child she named Hermaphroditus.

A fountain nymph fell in love with the youth

Hermaphroditus, but he spurned her. So she prayed to the gods for help, and they merged her with him, making him part man, part woman. No one he has since loved has ever returned his love.

Aphrodite blamed Father for their child's misery. It wasn't his fault, but that didn't stop her. She put a curse on his next child, who was born of the nymph Dryope, and who was me. Hermaphroditus is male and female. I am goat and god—because Aphrodite said Father behaved like a goat when he took her.

Like other gods, I can transform into whatever shape I wish. With one restriction: I can never transform into all god or all goat; neither half of me can ever be whole. Aphrodite thought this would mean I'd be lonely—for who could love a hybrid?

Aphrodite, the goddess of love, cursing someone to be unlovable—now there's a conundrum.

But the curse hasn't bothered me one bit. I'm never lonely. I am special among both gods and goats.

As for unrequited love, it can't happen without first falling in love, and I've never experienced the feeling. Father didn't need to warn me about getting "mixed up"—it just doesn't seem to be my nature. Both the male and female parts of the unfortunate Hermaphroditus yearn for love. But only my god half has any sense of what love is, and that is but an inkling. My goaty half enjoys the pleasures of many females without losing itself to any. So, the way I see it, Aphrodite did me a favor.

From nowhere returns a hint of the fear I felt after the female scorpion ate the male. Why? Why just now, when I'm thinking about love?

Ah, a warning—for the male was destroyed.

But I could never be destroyed by love.

A breeze comes up, carrying the scent of peonies. And salmon-colored cones of lupine blossoms to the right catch my eye as I prance. Yellow buttercups make a path for me, yellow like gold. Such a glorious day. I have to skip.

"Pan," sigh the quivering leaves. "Pan," murmur the tender buds. "Pan, you horned fellow, come play with us." The air wavers with giggles. "Come please us."

I should have known: The colors are so brash. "Sweet dryads," I call, spinning in a circle, "do you compete to win my attention?"

A face forms in the bark of a lone, tall oak. She smiles at me. "And why not? You handsome fellow."

Handsome. I pull on my patches of cheek fur. I am told that at my birth my own mother screamed and fled. My father accepted me joyfully and raised me on Mount Olympus. But my mother has never talked to me. Not once. "Do you sport with me yet again?" I say to the face in the tree. "Mating is no trifle."

"Don't be stern, Pan. Was it not you who sported with the scorpions a moment ago?"

So they were watching, nosy things. "I was repaying a debt."

"What debt can a lowly scorpion hold over a god?"

"Whatever debt I wish," I say with a smile.

The head and arms of the dryad emerge from the oak trunk. Her hair swings forward. "Have you no debt to me?"

"And to me?" Another lilting voice.

"And me?" A third. "We color your grounds. We perfume your airs. Dearest Pan, you who love nature most of all, you owe us heartily."

Dryads extend their hands from bushes all around. But the one in the tree lures me most. Her thighs begin to form from the bark, brown and strong and ready. I take a step toward her.

"So it's me? Good choice. Come."

I shouldn't. No nymphs—not the naiads of the waters nor the oreads of the mountains nor the dryads of the plants—no nymphs of any sort have ever received me even as a friend, much less as a lover.

"Handsome fellow," she calls in a warm voice.

I step forward.

"But wait, most welcome Pan." She holds up a hand. "Come to me in a new form, since it looks as if this day is destined for transformations."

I haven't the strength for another transformation. I should shake my head. But her toes peek from the bark. Small and kissable. Her ankles are slim. "What form?" I ask, my breath shallow.

"How about a man?" comes a voice from behind. "A nice big man, with legs and feet that have toes."

The nymphs know this is impossible. "Either half of me is better than a full man," I say.

"That's right," says the tree dryad. She smiles. "Ignore my sisters. You choose the shape, Pan." She lifts one graceful leg free from the tree. "You're the god, after all."

If only I could become a vine and wrap her tight to me. If only I could caress her with wide grape leaves, like so many hands, everywhere. But such precision takes more energy than I have.

"He's hesitating," says a voice.

"Completely out of juice," says another.

"What a simpleton he was to waste himself on the scorpion," comes a third voice. "Such a lowly creature."

"No creature is too lowly for the god of nature," says my dryad.

I can't tell whether she's mocking or wise. I wish I could understand her eyes. I can read thoughts in the eyes of any kind of creature except those I can never transform into. But I have to transform. I have to. For her.

Ah, I can play a well-known god trick.

I stretch my neck and chin to the heavens. I hold my arms out to both sides, fingers spread. All of me narrows, elongates—muscles and bones, hairs and teeth and hooves.

I become a sheet of water, glorious rain.

I sway forward to envelop the charming dryad. My spray wets her ruddy cheeks. Luscious maiden. My first nymph, my darling.

But this sensation is too fine, too wonderful; I can't hold the form.

She's already laughing. She counted on my being too excited to stay transformed.

I collapse into me, goat god, drenched and limp in the mud I caused.

The air rings with nymph laughter as I look up at the tree. All I see is bark.

"Very funny." I shake off the mud.

"Will he never learn?" comes a voice.

"Hopefully not." Another.

"You should have been Eros' child, little Pan," whispers the nymph of the oak, now totally hidden. "He's the god of love."

I puff out my chest. "Eros? Hermes has just as many conquests."

"Such a fool for love," says a nymph.

"You flatter yourselves, pretty maidens," I say. "There's a sea of difference between love and lust."

"Do you mean to say you don't love me?" comes the voice of my dryad. "Oh, boo-hoo. Poor little me."

"Lust or love," says another, "it doesn't matter. Pan is unlucky in both."

And they're laughing again.

I go on my way. They think they insult me, these maidens who pass their lives in plants. It's ludicrous. I'd tell them as much if I didn't pity their situation. They're boring, really, compared to maenads. Besides, maenads are honest and direct. You can trust a maenad, while all you can do with a nymph is wonder.

I head for the clearing, every part of me alert. A flock grazes this meadow. A ewe near the edge looks up, frightened. I have never understood how sheep can be so harebrained while goats are so curious and intelligent.

The ewe moves closer to the others, who chew their cud in contented companionship. Dull and slow, all of them.

"Yip yip yip yip yeeeeee!" I yell, and race through the flock.

They scatter in panic. Pan causes panic. That's what Father said last night.

I roll in the meadow, laughing.

chapter four

THE HUMAN

The midday heat bakes the earth and makes me yawn. Eternity is long; gods have a lot of empty time.

But then my eyes pop open, for a girlish voice zigzags about my ears.

The voice lilts closer.

I push up onto an elbow and look around.

A human child comes through the grasses. The gnarled olive branches filter the sun to silver. Shadow hides her face as she stoops to pick red and yellow and black anemones.

I scamper behind a thick tree trunk. Is she alone? How can that be? A girl child of her tender age shouldn't go unattended. Artemis, my most beloved aunt, protects maidens, especially when they romp in forests and meadows. Nevertheless, the girl's parents are neglectful to let her stray alone.

This part of Arcadia is sparsely populated. The only road runs from Argos, in the northeast, to ugly Sparta, in the central south. The difference between the two is like the difference between the sun and the moon. Which is she a child of?

I don't care for human adults, who scream when they see me.

But I like human children. I've watched them play, almost like goat kids. Nowhere near as nimble, though. On my two legs I can never run as fast as goats or climb with as much agility. But I can best any human at both.

I peek out from around the tree. The child talks to a flower.

She comes closer.

I pull my head out of sight. A long while passes. I scratch my rump against a low broken-off branch. A breeze shakes the narrow leaves, green-silver-green.

What is she doing?

I peek.

She rolls in the grass in full sunlight. Her hair picks up bits of stick and leaves. She's as blissful and free as some sort of cub.

I jump into view.

She gets to her feet, eyes instantly wet and bright, hands out to each side; at the first hint of evil, she'll take flight.

I sit on my haunches, thinking, Stay, child. Stay a while.

She bends at the waist just enough so that her face

comes forward slightly. Her small breasts press against her shift. She's older than I thought. "What are you?"

What, not who. She's taken me for a beast. She's an idiot, after all. The sharp points of my horns could pierce her soft belly like a knife through fresh cheese.

Her full face watches me, open, waiting.

And I see there is nothing dull in her eyes, nor any hint of superiority. Her purity deserves honesty. "A freak," I say.

She withdraws a step, blushing. She thinks I am embarrassed to be as I am. Silly girl. I am the delight of the gods.

"Do you mean me harm?" she asks.

"Never."

"Are you nasty like other hybrids?"

A nasty question. "Which hybrids do you speak of?"

"The centaurs," she says.

"Some centaurs are noble," I say.

"They're known for rape."

I shrug. "No, I'm not nasty."

Her arms lower slowly. She looks over her shoulder, then back at me. Her hands grip at the folds in her shift. And now I can see that she is a rare beauty.

I lift my nose and breathe deep. "You smell of thyme." A smell I favor; thyme honey is the best.

She touches her hair uncertainly and picks out debris. "Everything lives in these grasses."

"It's rash to roll here. You're lucky you aren't stinging from thistles."

"I checked first," she says. "None of these flowers or herbs is poisonous."

I grant her a small smile. "Who taught you so much about plants?"

"I learned on my own. I love the outdoors." She looks over her shoulder again.

"Are you expecting someone?" I ask.

She smiles shyly and shakes her head. "They don't know I took a walk. They forbid midday walks."

She could have said yes. She could have used a cloak of lies to protect herself. "And who are they?"

"My mother and sister and the servants. We stopped because of the heat, and Electra, she's my sister, she cried of thirst. Now they're napping."

"Did you cry?"

"I never cry."

I tilt my head. "You expect me to believe that?"

"Believe it or not, as you wish."

She's saucy. This time I hold in my smile. "I didn't mean to offend. Why would you refuse to cry?"

She hesitates. "Why should I answer you?"

"For the same reason I answer you."

She stands there silent.

I put both hands on my knees and rub my palms in circles. The knots of hair that form come off in clumps.

She picks one up. "Are you ill?"

I almost laugh. "Just molting."

She drops the clump and sucks in air. "Can you keep a secret?"

Why would this girl trust me so fast? I nod.

She looks at me hard. "I'm not my mother's daughter. Or, well, not her blood daughter. My real mother abandoned me at birth. So I have to be extra good to be loved. Before my sister was born, I didn't have to be so careful. But it's different now."

Her matter-of-factness steals my breath. A newborn abandoned by a mother—this is a story I know. Mothers can be cruel. After a moment, I ask in a quiet voice, "Why is this a secret?"

The girl shrugs.

"Do you know your real mother?" I ask.

"No."

I have to ask. "Do you know why she abandoned you?"

"She wasn't married."

"How do you know all this?"

"I overheard the servants, so I asked my mother."

"You asked her outright?"

"And why shouldn't I have?"

I smile. Her secret isn't much of a secret if all the servants know it. What a funny girl she is. "So what do you do when you're sad?"

"At home I compose a poem. A lyric poem, naturally. Euterpe, the muse of lyric poetry, is the best muse of them all."

I smile wider. The muses love to hear themselves praised. And now the air smells of violets, Euterpe's favorite flower, as though the muse herself is listening. "I love all the muses equally," I say, not to be diplomatic toward the others, but because it's true. They each have their own special ways.

"I don't. Anyway, if I'm out somewhere and I'm sad, then I just look around and drink the air."

I stand. "Are you thirsty?"

She looks at my legs and hooves with open curiosity, then back at my eyes. I might like this girl—this young woman. She smiles. "I didn't mean it that way, but yes. Mother gave all the water to Electra, because she's so small. She's only eight. I can wait till we get home."

"Home to Argos," I say.

"How did you know?"

"It had to be Argos or Sparta, and Sparta produces no poets. Warriors, yes. But those terrifying mountains and bitter lemon trees cannot foster poetry."

"Argos produces fine warriors, too." The girl puts her hands on her hips. "My father is one."

"Your real father or your adopted father?"

She sniffs and her face goes slack. "This is another secret. You must swear to keep this one as well."

"I swear."

"I don't know anything about my real father. The only man I know as father believes he is my real father. He was off in battle for months and months. When he returned home, my mother presented me to him as his own child."

Ah, a true secret, after all—the kind that everyone knows but the man of the household. How typical of humans. "And why do you keep this secret from him?"

"Mother asked me to. I don't know why. But I've never had to lie to him, because he's never asked, of course. It's good, because this way he loves me truly. Even more than he loves Electra. He says I am the fairer one."

Family deceit—an old story. I'm tired of it. "Come on." I turn and run.

The sound of her footsteps from behind spurs me to run faster. The meadow slopes downward and descents are hard on me; I have to slow or I'll trip and tumble the rest of the way.

"Where are we going?"

"Around that outcropping of rocks," I call back. "You'll see."

A lynx jumps from the top rock and she screams as the cat lands between us. He lunges onto her. She falls forward under the weight of the cat, curling, her face in her hands.

I charge from behind. My horns catch him in the flank and cut to the bone. He twists in agony. His forepaws grasp my left ankle.

Rocks pelt him. "Go away!" the girl shouts. She hurls another rock and growls. The girl growls!

I toss the beast free. He claws the air; I race at him and kick the back of his head. Blood spurts from the gash as he leaps away.

The girl stands rigid, another rock in her hand. "We're both alive."

I take the rock and throw it after the lynx. "You were brave to stay and fight."

"So were you." She whimpers and drops to the ground, clutching her calf.

I gently pry open her hands. She turns her head away. "The fangs sank in deep," I say, "but he didn't have enough time to rip away the flesh. It will heal well." If I can get the bad blood out, I'm thinking. That's what Asclepius, the healer, would do.

The girl hugs herself at first; then she puts her arms around my neck.

I jerk backward in hot surprise. She is more woman than I realized. How can she keep confusing me like this?

I lift her into my cradling arms. I can feel the pain in her ribs, where the lynx raked her, and in her leg, where he bit her. I feel it as though I'm the one bleeding.

The girl holds tight, and I carry her carefully, quickly, past the rocks to the stream. I wade to the center of the water and sit, so that we are both submerged to our necks. "This is where I was going to bring you before the lynx attacked."

A dragonfly shoots past in a blur of gauzy wings. It

hovers above the water at the riverbank. I remember the scorpions and my heart lurches.

The girl groans in pain.

I point to the dragonfly, hoping to distract her.

It catches a water-walker and flies away.

"Did you know that dragonflies can hunt only by day?" I ask.

The girl turns her face full to me. "Why?" Her eyes glow with intelligence.

"Because they fly so fast, they depend on good vision to keep them from colliding with things."

"I love knowing about nature."

"You growled at the lynx back there. Did you realize that?"

"That's what you're supposed to do," she says. "It scares them."

We look at each other and burst out laughing.

"I guess it was foolish." She shivers and pulls closer to me, her arms tighter on my neck. "It's pretty here—but it's cold."

I wish it were even colder. The water isn't nearly as cold as in spring, when the melting mountain snows overflow the banks. Not nearly cold enough to numb her wound. "I have to squeeze till your blood runs clean."

I lift her leg above the water and squeeze toward the wound, pressing from all sides. She flinches. Her blood flows like new wine. I lower the leg gently back into the water.

The girl's face is hard against my neck, lost in my beard. I cannot tell if she cries. And of course she wouldn't want me to know, this girl who never cries, who's never troublesome. Her hair brushes my lips. They pucker. I hold her close, almost in an embrace.

"Thank you," she says when she can finally manage to speak. "Are you a physician?"

"No, but I've learned much watching a fine one named Asclepius."

"Asclepius?" She pulls back from me a little. "He's the famous son of Apollo. He can raise the dead from Hades."

I smile. "You've heard of him? He's my friend."

She presses herself to me once again. "I'm so cold."

"Drink and we'll get out of the water."

"I'm not thirsty anymore."

"You will be later. Drink while you have the chance."

She straightens her arms and leans to the side for a drink, keeping her fingers clasped behind my neck. The need in those fingers feels good. A sudden doubt enters my head. "Can't you swim?"

She turns to me agian, her hair wet and shining. "I learned years ago. Even Electra swims. Father often takes us to Aulis, where the beaches are long and white. Someday I'll get married in Aulis."

My stomach tightens. Jealousy? "Are you betrothed already?"

She giggles. "No."

"Shouldn't you wait, then, to plan the wedding? Shouldn't you marry in the hometown of your husband?"

"Father is King of Argos. He says I can wed where I want. And Aulis is where I want."

Ah, so it was her mother's jewels that Father and I protected from the outlaws yesterday. I should have guessed this girl was royalty. That's why she seems so much younger than I know she must be—she's sheltered.

A princess. For a moment I'm impressed, and almost embarrassed that I don't know who the present King of Argos is. Humans die off too fast to keep track.

The girl looks dreamy. "I'll go barefoot on the sands."

I hate walking on sand. It rubs raw the soft pads on the undersides of my hooves—the pads that the scorpion poisoned one of just this morning. Those pads provide me a sure foothold when I climb uneven or slippery terrain. The beaches at Aulis would be unbearable for me.

"You can come and we can all dance," she says. "Are you a good dancer?"

I remember stumbling with the maenad this morning. I am the worst dancer, according to the muses. The worst dancer and the worst singer. But the girl is happy in her fantasy—and I do love to dance, despite my clumsiness. "I'd do my best to thrill you."

She laughs and her teeth chatter again. "Let's get out of the water now. Please. I have barely any feeling in my limbs."

I rise and carry her to the bank, setting her on her feet.

She shakes the water off, then flings her hair from side to side. It slaps her cheeks. "It's silly, but I feel colder out in the hot air." She shivers and jumps in place. "Ahi!" She grabs her calf. "It hurts so much."

"It will heal."

She points. "Will you heal?"

I look down at my left leg. The horny knob at the back above my hoof has been ripped away. The raw red patch seems strangely obscene. So it wasn't her pain I felt before; it was my own.

"It must hurt horribly." She puts her fingers to her lips. "Will it grow again?"

I shake my head.

She looks around anxiously. "What if the lynx comes back?"

"He won't. He must have been hungry beyond reason to attack anything as large as a human—especially when we were together. But he's hurt badly now. He's gone back to his lair to recover."

She clasps her upper arms and doesn't look convinced.

"Do you want me to carry you to your mother?" I turn and crouch, offering my back.

"Carry me? Even with your hurt?"

"Of course."

"I don't want to leave yet."

Nor do I. "Don't you want your mother to tend that bite?"

She looks at me with that look I saw before, when I asked her why she never cries—that look of resolve. She takes the hem of her shift, ripped by the lynx claws and totally soaked, and carefully peels the cloth up away from her skin until the bottom of her leg is exposed. She thrusts that leg toward me. "Will you lick it?"

I blink.

"Mother says animal spit makes wounds heal. I know you're going to lick your own leg. So lick mine, too." She hops forward on her good leg. "Please."

My face goes hot. "I'm not an animal."

"But you're half animal. That's why I told you my secrets—you promised to keep them and animals can't lie."

I can lie. I don't because I don't need to. But I won't tell her. She doesn't deserve to know.

She touches one of my horns. "You're half sheep."

"Goat," I say, in spite of myself. This conversation shouldn't be happening.

"Oh." She keeps her leg extended. "You have strange pointed ears. But otherwise your face is human."

"Not human. Numinous."

She scrunches up her nose. "What does that mean?"

"Godlike."

"My mother says the gods look just like humans. Anyway, why would you have a godlike face?"

I look away. Once humans know who I am, they become subservient, awestruck. "My father is Hermes."

The girl draws her leg away. "Herald and messenger of the gods, who travels with winged slippers?"

"No other."

She lets her wet skirt fall. "Are you an Olympian god, then?"

"I'm a minor god."

"I should have known. Midday is the most common time for encounters between gods and mortals. That's why I'm not supposed to be out and about now—it's dangerous." She rubs her forearms. "Male gods can be unscrupulous."

"You are bold to say that. And unwise."

She smiles and shrugs, and I can't help smiling back. "Can you play the lyre like Hermes?"

I can't remember Father ever playing a lyre. "No."

"Can you play other musical instruments?"

"No."

"That's a pity. Hermes played a golden lyre. Apollo let him become keeper of the herds in exchange for that lyre."

I've never heard about a lyre. I dig at the dirt with my right hoof. That she should know something about my father that I don't know!

"And then Hermes made a reed pipe and Apollo had his old nursemaids teach Hermes the art of divining by pebbles in exchange for the pipe."

"If Apollo took both my father's instruments, how could he teach me to play them?" I say quickly.

"You're right." She giggles. "Do you know how to read the future in pebbles?"

I begrudge this girl the answers to her infernal questions. This is far worse than her being awestruck. "No."

"Hmmm." She bobs her head. "I'd have expected Hermes to mate with a sheep or a cow, not a goat. It's sheep and cows he tended, after all."

At last something I know. "My mother was Dryope, the nymph."

The girl puts her fingertips together in a steeple. She appears pensive. "But if a nymph is your mother, why on earth are you half goat?"

"There are several hybrids," I say.

"Yes, like the centaurs. But they don't have a mother and father with ordinary human—or god—bodies."

"What about the Minotaur?"

The girl shakes her head. "The Minotaur's father was a real bull. That's not the same. When a god mates with a human or a nymph, the child has ordinary form, even if the god took on the form of an animal."

"You seem to know a lot about such things." My voice is cold.

"I should." She clears her throat. "When Zeus pursued Leda, the Queen of Sparta, he was at first a beaver, and then fiercer beasts, and finally a swan. A daughter, Helen, was hatched from her egg. She's my aunt. The half sister of my mother."

"I've heard of Helen. They say she is the fairest woman alive."

"She is. My mother is fair, too." Her yellow-flecked eyes shine like sun in trees.

It wasn't just my imagination; this girl is more beautiful than any human I have ever seen. "Do people say you look like your mother?"

"All the time. Isn't that funny? Everyone says I'll grow up to have the family beauty." The corners of her mouth hold the smallest trace of sadness. She hugs herself. "I'm sorry I asked you to lick my wound. I offended you."

Her voice is honey. And she looks at me so naturally, just as she'd look at anyone else. No other human has ever done that with me.

"It's all right," I say.

She limps to a patch of anemones and picks a handful. I watch as she patiently twists the stems together into garlands.

Her limp worries me. As soon as I've returned her to her mother, I'll rush to Asclepius for advice. I'll ask the physician about the wound to my ankle as well.

The girl comes back and stands on tiptoe before me, a garland dangling from each hand. I don't dare to move.

She hangs the garlands over my horns, then steps back and smiles approvingly.

I am lost in her admiring eyes. What fortune led me to meet this wonderful girl?

“My leg hurts,” she says in a quiet voice. “Will you still carry me back?”

I squat.

“It’s too bad you’re a god.” She climbs on. “You’d have made the best pet.”

chapter five

HOOVED ANIMALS

I should go to Asclepius and ask if I did the right thing for the girl's wound. I should ask him to intervene so that she recovers fast.

This was my plan.

Until the girl said I would have made the best pet.

So, instead, I sit on a boulder and watch a lynx devour a fawn out in the middle of a clearing. It is the same lynx my horns gouged. Amazing. His hunger must be savage for him to be out and about with that pain.

My own injury has stopped hurting, but when I look at the back of my left ankle, the bareness where my knob used to be makes me quiver. I feel marked.

The goddess Artemis appears beside my rock. She is weeping.

I leap to the ground. "Goddess of nature, goddess of night, dearest aunt, what brings tears to your lovely eyes?"

"The fawn." Artemis looks at the lynx ravaging the small carcass, then lets her head fall toward me. Her fingers comb my beard affectionately. Her brown cheeks shine wet as the early glow of summer moonlight mixes with the brilliance of the afternoon sun. Of all animals, deer are her favorite. "This is the fault of that wretched girl you were with."

"Have I heard right?" I gasp. "You are the protector of maidens. Would you really rather the lynx had killed the girl than the fawn?"

A doe paws the ground near the boulder. I recognize her as Taugete, the daughter of Atlas whom Heracles desired. Artemis turned her into a deer to save her from his pursuit. Her udder is full to bursting. She looks at me with one liquid eye, and I know immediately: This fawn was hers. What fierce suffering.

"That girl is trouble, Pan," says Artemis.

"No. Blame me. I'm the one who stopped the lynx, dearest aunt. The girl was powerless against him."

"And you were powerless against the girl, so it all comes back to her."

"No—"

Artemis' hand claps my mouth shut. "It's the girl's fault." She turns and walks away with the doe.

Her absence makes the area feel deserted. Not even a bird calls.

Powerless against that girl? Me?

She left hours ago. She begged me to go all the way back with her. She claimed her mother would want to thank me for saving her life. When I thought about her mother's likely reception of me and laughed aloud, she just said her leg hurt far too much—I simply had to carry her right up to the door of the carriage. But I'd have nothing to do with that excuse, either.

When we were close enough, I set her on the ground and walked away without looking back. I left her, the way Artemis has left me now.

But I heard her mother call, "Iphigenia."

Iphigenia: a poet at heart, who talks to flowers, who knows the plants. She's honest. So she's about as good as humans get. Yet she said such a stupid thing.

I am nothing like a pet.

Humans are dullards. I'm lucky to be rid of this one—what a buffoon I was to be taken in by her beauty. By her futile act of throwing rocks at a lynx to protect me.

Artemis is right: a curse on Iphigenia.

I walk to the stream where I washed her wound. I drink, then spit.

Me, a pet. Me, the one all the gods love.

I hate humans.

What I need now is to play with a herd of mountain goats.

I'm already running up a hill to the nearest salt lick. The sour smell of a herd ahead lures me and I burst upon them.

The group stampedes in surprise, bouncing off one another in their haste. Gone.

"That's all right," I say, panting. I can wait and then approach slowly. They'll accept me. They're not stupid, like sheep.

Iphigenia thought I was half sheep.

Stop that. Forget the girl.

I drop to my knees, exhausted. Mindlessly, I lick at the salt.

I don't know what I'm doing here. And I don't care. I feel . . . sad. It's not like me. I'm Pan. I play.

What a long day, and all of it wrong.

The late sun still beats down. I stand and search for shade.

I spy a rock ledge that forms an overhang. Three goats lie there. Nannies.

I approach gingerly.

The closest one lifts her head and regards me. The twitch of her tail tells me she has recognized my maleness.

I stop.

She flops back down. Her bottom jaw moves in a circle, chewing chewing.

I wait, resting on my haunches.

After a while, the nanny props herself up on one foreleg and paws the earth with the other, to give herself a dust bath.

I stand and walk closer. "Itchy," I say. "I know how it is. I will finish my own molting within the next moon."

She stops moving and watches me with one eye.

Even a whisper from a maenad or a nymph can get me going, but I've never been aroused by a nanny.

A storm clouds the eastern sky, despite the beating sun. The air turns sharp. My hairs stand on end.

The nanny is absolutely still.

"Nanny, imagine this." I whisper now. "Imagine a girl taking you as her pet. Imagine her thinking she can tame you."

A fly lands on the goat's shoulder. The muscles tense under her coat, then release. Her eyelid closes halfway.

Oh, just for a while I'd like to be all goat, to belong here. When I was a child, eons ago, I loved to play with goat kids, though they climbed higher and faster than I ever could. I'd forgotten all those old feelings. But in this moment I long to transform into full goat, to be whole for a little while. Not special. Just plain.

True belonging. Respite.

I take the flower garlands from my horns, the ones Iphigenia made for me, and toss them near the nanny. "Eat up."

The nanny jumps to her hooves, knocking me to the ground, and kicks me in the thigh. The other two nannies also stand close together, at the ready.

I laugh out loud, despite the pain in my thigh.

The youngest of them advances, threateningly.

I hobble downhill fast, and, ahiii! I trip and fly, head over hooves. Sharp rocks gouge my sides and back, my hands flail, and I land, my face smashed in anemones. The wind of the approaching storm ruffles through my fur, chilling me.

The flowers I lie in are blood red. Like the blood of the fawn in the lynx's mouth.

These flowers are a message from Artemis. She mourns the fawn's death. Is she telling me not to risk her anger further? I shiver now. I love Artemis best of all my aunts; we never quarrel.

The west wind picks up. All at once the sun shines, the storm clouds are pushed away, and the syrup smell of myrtle fills my mouth. I look up. The branches of a myrtle in full bloom spread over me. The myrtle is Aphrodite's tree. A single dove warbles near the top, Aphrodite's bird.

So it's not just Artemis who speaks to me today; Aphrodite has her part, too. Aphrodite—the source of my curse.

It all comes together.

Does Aphrodite think I'm an idiot?

Iphigenia was picking anemones when I first saw her. Red and black and yellow. The garlands she made were of anemones. Things come together in confusing ways, but I sense a trick. Aphrodite must have lured the girl to the meadow with those flowers. She put the girl before me. Of course. She knew the girl was unique—innocent as an egg. She knew I'd be charmed. She's trying to get me to love this human—this beauty who will never return my love.

Well, Aphrodite won't get her way this time. The girl made a fool of me; I will never love her. I shouldn't even have carried her back to her carriage.

I squat and bite my knee in self-reproach.

chapter six

THE MUSES

After I figured out the message of the anemones, I knew that Artemis had to be expecting me. I sought her for a week, to beg her forgiveness; I was truly sad for Taugete's loss. Since Arcadia is Artemis' favorite haunt, I should have found the moon goddess quickly. But I failed.

So now I'm going in search of Aphrodite, who is probably on the island of Cyprus. I've got to do something to calm her down. The journey on land will take me north and across to the other side of the Aegean Sea and, since Mount Olympus is on the way, I'm stopping here to see Father.

A woman runs laughing on the mountain up ahead, clothed in gauze, a ring of flowers around her neck. Hooray. There they are, the muses, all nine of them wreathed in flowers, like the garlands Iphigenia wove for me.

Stop. Stop thinking about that girl.

I think instead about the unlikelihood of finding the muses here. They play on the mountains of Pierus and Helicon and Parnassus much more often than on Olympus. "What luck brings you here today?" I call out.

"Pan!" Clio, the muse of history, almost floats toward me, she is so tenuous and airy. "Dear sweet Pan." She stoops to pick sprigs of burnt-orange knotweed and tucks them behind my ears.

The image of Iphigenia invades my head. She, too, decorated me.

"We've come to sing with Apollo," says Polyhymnia. She smiles shyly and steps out from behind her sister to twist more knotweed spikes around my horns.

"And to dance to his lyre." Terpsichore twirls toward me, around me.

Apollo's lyre—the one Iphigenia said used to belong to my father.

"We'll even let you dance, clumsy little Pan. I'll give you lessons." With her slender toes, Terpsichore taps the side of my hoof.

My ears burn at the word *clumsy*. When the dancing begins, I'm drawn to it, but all I can do is trip. I'd be the bumpkin at Iphigenia's wedding.

Stop it. No more about that infuriating girl.

"And we'll amuse you with poetry," says Euterpe, the muse of lyric poetry—the kind Iphigenia composes. She kisses me on the cheek, warmly, as though we have a special bond.

Erato pushes her aside. "You're ready for all kinds of poetry, Pan, not just lyric." Her eyes tease: Erato's poetry is about desire. She tickles around the base of my horns.

And with that one little act, I'm caught—goaty me. All thoughts of troubles scatter. We move nimbly up the mountain, the ten of us together.

"Pan!" Apollo shouts in greeting, his arms open wide, his face a sunburst of joy. "No sight could please me more."

We settle on a smooth mosaic floor and drink nectar from red porcelain bowls, while the muse Urania tells how the constellations of the bears came to be.

Usually the start of storytelling is my cue to run off; I have too much energy to lie still and listen. But today I let myself be carried by Urania's words. She's a better storyteller than Iphigenia. And if I bide my time, I might get the chance to talk with Apollo alone before climbing higher to find Father.

Urania's warm voice paints the air. She tells of the nymph Callisto, who bore a son to Zeus and then was turned into a bear by Zeus' outraged wife, Hera. When the boy grew up, he went hunting and came upon the bear who was his mother. Zeus snatched Callisto away just in time and put her in the sky as a constellation. "A tragedy was avoided," says Urania. She folds her hands into her lap, finished.

Erato taps me on the knee. "My turn," she says with a sly look.

"But no," says Melpomene, the muse of tragedy. "It's my turn."

"No more tales of family killings, or near-killings." Apollo's command surprises all of us. He puts a sprig of laurel leaves into his mouth. "Tell, instead, of love thwarted. Amuse us, dear muse."

The odor of the fresh laurel he chews permeates the air. Love thwarted. I can't help but think of one of the few tales I know—about Daphne, who was turned into a laurel tree to escape Apollo.

"As you wish," says Melpomene. "Hear the tale of a mulberry tree and a lion's bloody mouth, a tale of doomed love." Her voice flows with sorrow.

I'm not listening anymore. My mind is on the bloody mouth of the lynx that attacked Iphigenia, then ate the fawn of Taugete. I remember Artemis saying, "It's the girl's fault." I need to speak with Artemis as well as Aphrodite. First thing in the morning.

Melpomene has finished her tale, so Apollo prepares to play his lyre.

"Uncle?" I walk to his side. "Teach me to play." My voice is steady; it doesn't betray how hard my heart beats.

Apollo cocks his head. "Why?"

It's my right. That very lyre on Apollo's lap was made by my father.

But before I can speak, Erato leans between our shoulders from behind. "Music is the language of seduction. Who's your prey, Pan?"

The other muses cast off their sad faces. They giggle and come close.

"Lechery?" says Clio.

I smile and feign a leer at all of them.

"One of us?" asks Terpsichore, batting her eyelashes.

More giggles.

"You don't fool me," says Thalia, muse of comedy. "I saw you with that nanny. A minute more and you'd have been mounting her."

The muses' giggles turn to laughter and Apollo rolls onto his back in a fit of guffaws.

So Thalia watched me. I stand and stretch, trying to appear at ease. "I'm going to find my father now."

"Relax, sweet Pan," says Clio, pushing down on my shoulders. "Hermes is in Athens. It's the fourth day of the month."

The Athenians make sacrifices to Hermes on the fourth of every month. He may very well be eating a sacrificed nanny right now. My stomach turns. How could I have lost track of the days and come at so inopportune a time? I squat again.

"Let's hear more about this object of your desires," says Erato. "So it's not a goat."

"A human, then?" asks Melpomene. "Gods and humans always make for good tragedy. Who is she?"

"I saw you with a human not long ago," says Euterpe. She puts her palms together and presses the tips of her fingers to her chin. "I was in Arcadia, and I saw you with Iphigenia. Such a fine girl. So discerning."

I remember Iphigenia's praise of Euterpe. The air smelled of violets. I suspected then that Euterpe was there. I didn't mind it at the time, but now I'm angry that we were spied on. Both Euterpe and Thalia. It's too much.

"Do you mean the daughter of Helen?" Apollo puts his arm around my shoulder. "Were you with that stunning girl?"

"Helen is her aunt, not her mother," I say without emotion, though his words make my insides churn. Apollo is the most handsome of gods; he can charm any human he wants.

"Not so," says Apollo. "When Helen was ten years old, Theseus stole her away from Sparta. He brought her to his mother in Attica. Years later, her brothers rescued her. She gave birth to Theseus' child soon after. But she was too young to care for a baby. So her married sister raised the baby as her own."

"Your Iphigenia is daughter to the most beautiful human woman in the world," says Erato. "No wonder you're entranced."

"She's not mine," I say quickly. "And I'm not entranced."

"Apollo's right," says Clio, ignoring me. "She's quite a

beauty in her own right. Her beauty might well surpass her mother's when she's fully grown."

"Is that what you want, Pan?" asks Erato. "A beautiful human?"

"Don't encourage him," says Melpomene.

"I didn't say I wanted her."

Apollo gives me a sharp look. "Be careful, Pan. Humans are fickle."

"Fickle?" says Thalia. "This from the god who pursued Marpessa and Coronis and Creousa and Cyrene and Melia." She counts off the names on her fingers. "And Euadne and Thero and Psamathe and Philonis and Chrysothemis. Look, I've run out of fingers and I'm not done yet."

"Can Apollo help it if human women find him irresistible?" Erato laughs. "Pan just wants what Apollo has."

"Don't confuse things," says Apollo. "I'm a prize to look at. Human women won't react the same way to Pan. They won't love him back."

Everyone hushes. Euterpe sucks in her breath loudly. All the muses are looking at me. The worry in their faces puts a tightness in my own chest in spite of myself. They are afraid that I suffer because of Aphrodite's curse—afraid that, yes, I am unlovable.

How can they think that? Don't they love me?

Of course they do.

But not romantically. Not a one of them has ever invited me into that kind of embrace.

I cannot speak.

Erato clears her throat. "Love?" She taps her fingers lightly on her lips. "I thought we were talking about lust. That's what Pan said to the dryads, after all."

So she was there when the dryad teased me. "Have all of you been spying on me?"

"Watching over you, not spying," says Thalia. "Hermes asked us to."

What a stupid thing for Father to do. "Well, stop it," I say. "I don't need watching over."

"That's right, Pan." Erato turns her wrist quickly, as though tossing trash. "Take care of yourself. Forget love. Have fun. The pleasure is as good—and love carries pain where lust does not."

"Love is an absurdity, anyway," says Apollo.

"An absurdity that humans make into fine tragedy, however," says Melpomene.

Apollo harrumphs. "Humans moan and groan over it; their lives are short. They can dedicate themselves to suffering. But to us gods, treating love seriously is the greatest joke. Nothing that intense could last an eternity." He looks directly at me.

I want to shout that I don't care one bit about that kind of love, I don't, I don't. I want to shout because I'm being lectured to and the muses aren't acting right and nothing feels as it should.

Before I can find the words, Terpsichore says, "How true," and, with a sigh, "Dear Pan."

"Silly little Pan," says Calliope, coming from behind me.

Thalia moves to my side.

They run their hands over my head, down my back.

They are petting me. One after the other.

So I am the best pet. I am the pet of the gods. Every last one.

I jump up and stomp to the nearest pine. I shake the knotweed from behind my ears and sweep it off my horns. Clio and Polyhymnia, the ones who decorated me, take each other's hand. All of them watch, hushed, even Apollo. I fashion myself a garland of pine, of sharp needles, deep green, nothing fancy or refined. It suits me. Anyone who tries to pet me will get their fingers pricked.

chapter seven

SYRINX

The rubble around me was once a temple, but an earthquake destroyed it. Nevertheless, the farmers come here to sit and think. Sometimes they stage games in front of these ruins. Races on foot, or on horseback, or in chariots; the discus throw and archery and wrestling.

I follow the stone steps up to a platform surrounded by fallen columns. Miniature daisies peek out between the stones, and tall yellow and red spikes of kniphofia offer nectar to bees. The autumn light falls like rain and a lone scorpion skitters by, defying the change of seasons.

The scorpion brings back that day with Iphigenia, that spring day half a year ago that still haunts me. I replay our time together, her words. It's become an obsession; sometimes I feel ill with it.

Iphigenia is the most fascinating human I know because

she is the only human I've had a true conversation with. Her beauty overwhelms me because she inherits her mother's—no man, even someone experienced with human women, could fail to succumb. Anyone would await her womanhood breathless.

This is not love. This is infatuation. And it's contrived by my enemy, Aphrodite.

But then I think again of the girl's words, of how she does not cry. Of all that means.

Iphigenia hid nothing from me. That's what I value most in her.

But she did it because she thought I was an animal and so couldn't dissemble. A twisted gift, her honesty.

Still, she stayed honest and vulnerable even after she found out I was a god. And she made me see how others see me. A painful gift, but a precious one.

I think these things as I walk. I think in spirals.

Mount Lycaeus rises behind me. I've been climbing mountain after mountain for months, always in Arcadia. After my visit to Olympus, I gave up the idea of going to Cyprus. Artemis cannot possibly hold a grudge against me, we understand each other so well. And there's no way I could appease Aphrodite, anyway. So I have decided to stay away from the gods. All of them. I'm no one's pet.

These are my hills and mountains. Every rock, every plant accepts me. The lizards and snakes, the insects and arachnids, the most lowly creatures—they accept me without surprise. I avoid all others.

I start the climb now, comforted by the beauty of this land. The air is thin and clean. I breathe deeply and realize there's no trace of goat here. The bushes at the base of the mountain show no sign of the browsing of goat herds.

"Oh!" A brown maiden stands in the bushes, glowing with health and strength. Is it Artemis at last?

I come forward. "So you came looking for me?"

"Stop." The maid flushes and clutches the bowl in her arms against her belly. I cannot glimpse what she's been gathering, but I can see her face clearly now. I don't recognize her after all. "Are you a satyr?" she asks. "Because if you are, I warn you now, take heed. I am the wood nymph Syrinx, and Artemis will not stand for any of us to be violated in these mountains."

"I believe you." I put up my hands against her outburst. I crouch small.

She breathes hard through her nose.

"It's funny you should talk of Artemis," I say. "I took you for her at first."

Syrinx presses her lips together. Her eyes dart here and there, searching for an escape route.

"I'm no satyr," I say in a gentle, reasonable tone that is as far from the drunken raucousness of a satyr as anyone could imagine. "If I were, all I'd have to do is smite the ground and you, like any other nymph, would be forced to obey me. But I sit here and obey you instead."

She seems to ease a little, but she doesn't speak.

"You've introduced yourself, lovely Syrinx. Now it's my turn. I'm Pan."

Her mouth curves slowly with relief. "I've heard about you."

"I, on the other hand, know nothing of you."

She blinks. A breeze ruffles her hair like tiny rapids in a river.

And suddenly the words bubble from me: "I do know something of you, after all. You will live with water all around."

"How do you know this?"

"Your hair told me."

Syrinx frowns and tightens her lips. She squares her shoulders. "Why do you wear a garland of pine needles on your head?"

I straighten the garland with one hand. "I like pine. Now it's your turn: What's in the bowl?"

Syrinx flips it bottom up. Purple globes of thistle flower fall. Violets flutter after them. Early-evening moths swirl around the pile at Syrinx' feet.

"I like flowers, too." I pick a violet and hold it out to her. "Do you know that some of them taste good?"

Syrinx looks at the flower in my hand. Her fingers move rapidly, fluttering like the flowers she dropped. Then she smiles small. "I eat violets all the time." She lowers her head almost coyly. "Have you tasted daylilies?"

I nod. "And pansies."

"And their cousin heartsease." She laughs.

"You'd make a good grazer," I say.

"Did you come here to graze?"

Is that an insult? Or have I become too quick to find offense these days?—for the clarity of her voice tells me it's not. "I came to explore."

She looks back at me. Then she points beyond me.

I turn and see it; a large wolf watches from a distance. "He's out and about at an odd hour," I say.

"Wolves are always out on Mount Lycaeus. Alone or in packs. You can't help but see them. They never bother anyone," she says softly. "They just watch."

She skips down the stone steps, then slows and turns her head just slightly, like a queen. Something in the way she does it tells me she's interested in me. It's not flirting or teasing as other nymphs do with me—it's more like the way Iphigenia looked at me. She wants me to appreciate her—to recognize what she knows.

I sense the way her heart speeds when she thinks of the wolves watching her. I pick up a stick and toss it toward the wolf. The beast races off. "Do you like that?"

She stops walking. "What do you mean?"

"Do you like knowing the wolves watch you?"

"What are you suggesting?" Her eyes flash. She flicks the back of her hand against one of my horns. "You're impertinent."

"I just want to understand you."

"I've got to go now." She walks quickly into the woods.

"Syrinx," I call, staying close behind her. "Please stay and talk a while."

"There's nothing to talk about."

"Tell me stories, then."

She looks over her shoulder. "Do you mock me?"

"Never."

"Anyone who plays with the gods knows more stories than a simple nymph knows."

"Anyone who listened, perhaps. I have a lot of catching up to do." I run now and catch up to Syrinx as if my action will prove my words.

"You're telling the truth, aren't you?" Syrinx slows down and regards me thoughtfully. "I do know a lot of tales." She smiles uncertainly. "What are you interested in hearing about?"

Her question takes me by surprise, and so does my answer: "Why—how nymphs see things."

She blinks. "What do you mean?"

"It's just that my mother is a nymph—and I've never met her."

"And who is your mother?"

"Dryope. My father, one of the gods, came to her on Mount Oeta."

"Oh. But why . . ." Syrinx looks at me, then rushes ahead.

I skip beside her. "Why what?"

"Why should a child of Apollo be half goat?"

"What are you talking about? I'm not Apollo's son."

"But Apollo came to Dryope in the form of a tortoise. She picked him up and held him to her bosom, and he transformed into a snake and had his way with her."

I grab Syrinx by the arm. How many gods had their way with my mother? "Are you sure of this?"

"And you're her son. . . . Oh." She puts her free hand to her mouth. "I got confused. Apollo didn't lead to a son, Hermes did. You're Hermes' child, the one Dryope's worried about."

"Worried?" My hand tightens on Syrinx' arm. "Do you know my mother?"

"I shouldn't have said anything. Forgive me."

"Speak."

She shakes her head and tries to pull free. "Let go."

"Tell me everything," I say.

Her eyes grow frantic. She yanks her arm away and runs.

I stand a moment, looking at the spot where she stood. It is empty. My hand is empty. I run after her. "Wait!"

Syrinx runs faster. She trips over roots and her bowl falls and cracks. She scrambles to her feet and leaves the bowl behind, running running.

"Please wait," I call.

She runs with a swiftness that cannot be natural. A numinous force must be helping her. But why? All I want is to talk with her, to hear what she knows of my mother. My mother who worries about her son. Me. Syrinx runs ever faster.

I don't know these woods well, but the quiet tells me we're nearing the River Ladon. Syrinx splashes in among the reeds, and startled ducks take to the air noisily. The nymph cries out, "It's too deep. I can't cross. Oh, please, please, save me from this abomination."

"Don't be alarmed," I call as I sink into the sandy bank. I jump into the water. "Give me your hand. All I want is to talk."

"Liar. You're just like Apollo after all," Syrinx says. "Oh, Daphne, oh, my nymph sisters, help me." She splashes in deeper, her arms flying over her head.

I sense her total panic, as though I am Syrinx, as though I fear for my own virtue. "I won't hurt you," I cry.

I leap and reach out to pull her to safety. My hands close around hers. Alas, no, my hands hold nothing but reeds. As I watch, her arms, as well, turn to reeds, her body lengthens and thins to reeds, her hair mats into the tufts of the bulrushes. Syrinx is no more.

Oh, woeful world.

This is how Daphne escaped Apollo—her father, the river god Peneus, turned her into a laurel tree. And Apollo fouls her memory by chewing laurel leaves.

I had no base intentions against Syrinx. I am nothing like Apollo. I am not his son. I take pleasure in the maenads, who welcome me. I have never taken gifts not offered. I don't need to steal. I am Pan, god of nature, strong and sure.

And look what harm stealing does. How much Syrinx has lost, how much Daphne lost, how much so many nymphs and humans have lost at the hands of ruthless gods. I feel it as though I am each one of them.

No! I am nothing nothing nothing like Apollo.

But, yes, I am. I am thoughtless like him. I should have expected Syrinx to run; her fear was palpable. I never should have chased her.

Poor Syrinx.

Stupid me.

I sink to my knees. The reeds snap off in my hands. These are the fingers of Syrinx. I clutch them and cry.

chapter eight

ASCLEPIUS

Hours later I'm still lying out in the open, moaning in misery, like a beast, with Syrinx' reed fingers in a pile beside me. My head hurts from sadness.

Caw! A raven takes to the air in alarm as a serpent creeps over the lip of the wide ledge where I lie.

I jump up.

Another serpent follows. These aren't the venomous kind, but the kind that writhe in the temple at Epidaurus—the temple of the healer, my friend Asclepius.

I run to the edge and look down Mount Lycaeus. "Asclepius! Is it you?"

The thin man leans on a walking stick, close to the end of his strength, but his smile is generous. "Salutations, Pan." A line of serpents follows as far as I can see, back into the woods.

Another raven screams from a treetop before taking to the air.

I rush to him and hug him close. "Your entourage has scared away the ravens."

"No one needs ravens."

"Why would you say that?" I ask.

"It was the raven that robbed me of my mother."

I knew how Asclepius was raised, but I never wondered why. Mothers often don't raise their young—like my mother, like Iphigenia's mother. I drape my arm across his shoulders. "I am ready for stories these days," I say. "Tell me."

"My mother was the human Coronis. She was pregnant by Apollo when she made the mistake of taking another lover. Apollo's favorite bird, the white raven, reported on her infidelity. In a rage, Apollo turned the bird black." Asclepius looks into the woods as though scanning the area for more ravens.

"The poor raven was nothing more than a messenger," I say.

"The messenger deserved the punishment this time. How could he not predict the ugly path Apollo's wrath would take? Apollo had his twin sister, Artemis, shoot a quiver of arrows into the doomed woman. But as the flames of the funeral pyre licked Coronis' legs, Apollo came to his senses and tried to save her. It was too late. While Apollo cried, Hermes sprang into action: He snatched me from Coronis' womb and gave me to the centaur Chiron to raise."

Apollo killed the mother of his own son. This god who can't stand tales of family killings. I squeeze Asclepius' shoulders. "Your father was too harsh."

"But Hermes was wise. If I hadn't been raised and trained by Chiron, I wouldn't know how to heal."

"My father, Hermes, did well by you."

"Yes. And your father sent me now."

I shake my head. "But why?"

"You're in pain. He said you cried."

So Father has been spying on me now, too. Why did he not reveal himself? And how stupid he is—I don't need a surgeon. "Not physical pain, Asclepius. Come." I lead him to the ledge and gather the reed fingers into my hands. "I chased the nymph Syrinx. She turned into river reeds to escape me."

"There are plenty of others to roll with, Pan."

"That's not what makes me cry. Not at all. What's awful is her fate."

Asclepius sinks to his knees and sits back on his heels. "This is a tale like many others—gods chase nymphs, nymphs meet harsh fates. This sort of thing never troubles any god."

"It troubles me."

"How can it? You went after her, Pan."

"All I wanted was to talk, but she thought it was an assault."

"Well, then, it wasn't your fault."

"Does that matter? What I did changed her life forever."

Asclepius leans toward me. "You're truly upset."

"Asclepius, something strange happened. I felt Syrinx' terror as she ran from me. I felt it as though it were my own."

"Look at it as a gift, Pan."

"A gift? No. For now I feel Syrinx' despair."

"Let me see those." Asclepius holds out the cup of his hands. I pour in the reeds. He fingers them tenderly. "Tell me about the river these new reeds grow in."

"It's the sandy Ladon."

Asclepius nods. "Describe it."

"At this time of year it's wide. Bulrushes and cattails and reeds line the sides."

"Syrinx has plenty of company," says Asclepius. "She won't be lonely."

"But in winter, the river plants die back. Syrinx will sink into the shallow water, into the mud."

Asclepius sets the reeds on the ground and lines up each piece, side by side. "Do you know why I keep snakes in my temple?"

"To scare away ravens?"

Asclepius laughs. "Come rest your head."

I lie on my back with my head on his lap. Instantly I realize how exhausted I am.

Asclepius massages my forehead, my temples. "You've

recently molted. Your skin is smooth as oil. My snakes are smooth, too. They slough their skins every year, renewing hope." His long fingers press along the base of my skull.

"Spring is like that," I say slowly, struggling to stay awake. "That's what you mean, isn't it? Spring on the river will bring rushing waters and new plants from the shoots of the old."

"A renewed Syrinx, every year."

"That's not enough, Asclepius. When she talked, her voice carried me away. I wanted to listen to her all day. And . . ." I stop and swallow.

"What, Pan? What else?"

"She treated me differently from the way other nymphs do. She talked to me as though she cared about what I thought of her. Until I scared her, I think she was interested to know me."

"Why shouldn't she be?"

Asclepius doesn't see how others treat me. "I'm lucky to know you, Asclepius."

"No more lucky than I am to know you."

"Syrinx was a beautiful girl, playing in nature. She deserves better than to be a rooted, silent reed, no matter how many springs bring her rebirth. I owe her more than that."

Asclepius' fingers knead the muscles where my neck meets my shoulders.

I wake to morning sun, and the image on the undersides of my eyelids disappears, a maiden ensnared in despair. She is snatched from me, her face unseen. But it wasn't a nymph; it wasn't Syrinx. And, of course, I don't need the face to know who it was; I know too well who it was. Iphigenia. My mind scrambles absurdly.

Welcome, Daylight, who banishes my foolishness.

But, alas, my open eyes take in my solitude: Asclepius is gone, back to Pergamus.

I stretch, and accidentally scatter the reeds. They roll and smack one another with light clicks. A few tumble off the rock, lost down the mountainside. I pick one up. Overnight the reeds have dried stiff.

And hollow.

I work my pinky finger down the inside of each reed, twisting to get out loose fibers. There are seven reeds left. I laugh in grateful wonder; seven notes form the harmony of the heavens.

I must do this right. I must do it in a way worthy of Syrinx.

I blow down each reed, nibbling at one end to make them exactly the right lengths. My ear is good—something Iphigenia has made me see as a gift from Father. A rill runs nearby. I wash the finished reeds in the clear sweet water, then bring them back to the rock.

While the reeds bake in the sun, I go searching, ears erect. The morning whispers many melodies, but there's only one I seek. And there it is: *buzz.*

I follow the honeybee to the brown bumpy sack that hangs in an ancient olive tree. Only a few bees crawl on the outside of the hive.

I wish I could apologize to the bees. I climb the tree in silence, poked and scraped by branches. I reach out and swipe the hive, then drop to the ground and run, clutching it.

A tiny army of bees pursues me, so I turn and let out the scream that scatters sheep.

The bees circle each other in confusion, then fly back toward the olive tree.

My hands hesitate on the hive full of bee grubs. But a swift death is best, so I crush it. A crippled worker bee hidden inside hobbles toward my thumb. I don't stop her. The sting is sharp.

When I get to the ledge, I rub a section of rock clean, then place the hive there. I press on it over and over, picking out bits of leaf and twig that have stuck to the outside, kneading the beeswax uniform and golden. Now I join the reeds together with the wax, arranging them by length.

A reed flute.

My reed flute.

I walk to the River Ladon. "Listen, Syrinx. Please. Accept my offering."

I put the flute to my lips, and I hear Iphigenia's voice asking me about music, about what music I can make. I blow. After many tries, the notes come clear and as piercingly tender as Syrinx' voice. But the songs I make up are rough. Harmony is what I lack now, what I need so much.

What a fool I am, to think I can simply pick up a flute and make music like my father. Asclepius said Chiron trained him to become the physician that he is.

I can become the musician I want to be, the musician Syrinx deserves.

I wash my face in the river and lean reverently toward the reeds. "I promise, Syrinx, I'll master this flute."

part two

MUSIC

chapter nine

CHANGES

The snow has melted except on the most sheltered mountain crevices, the ones that face north. It is the start of spring. Mud and burrs dirty my winter coat so that it's hard to see its real color, moonlight silver. I comb out knots with my fingers, yank at the larger ones.

I'm awake and I don't know why. The middle of the day should be my sleep time. I get up and walk out of my cave into the sunshine. I listen. Nothing. I didn't really expect to hear anything; the shepherds in this area have come to respect my nap. Or perhaps they fear me. Last autumn I shouted at one who woke me, and he dropped his whistle and ran for dear life. I laughed and called out, but he was already too far away to hear.

Maybe they call me the crabby god, those shepherds. Pan, the one who strikes panic into their hearts, as I used to do with the sheep just for fun. But I don't care. Here the gods don't come looking for me. Good. I'd rather be known as an ill-tempered hermit than the pet of the gods. I don't miss a single one of them. Not even Artemis. Not even Father.

Nature is all I want or need. This particular mountain is a good place; full of wild goats, who are incapable of trickery. I like knowing they are close.

The bleat of a nanny comes faintly. I spy her, alone on a rock ledge that reflects the light. She bends her back legs just a little and a white kid drops. So early. This must be the first birth of spring. The newborn lifts his head on an unsteady neck. His narrow ears work free from his sticky head and pop out to each side, stiff and strange. He struggles to his feet and staggers. I'm smiling at his sweetness, grateful to whatever it was that woke me to witness this.

From nowhere an eagle swoops and carries off the newborn. The nanny looks around in astonishment. I throw my head back and scream at the bird, at the sky, at the gods. The nanny bolts for higher ground. Where is her herd? They should have surrounded her, kept the newborn safe until the mother found her bearings again.

I leap up the mountainside. A dozen females cluster in a small mountain meadow. "Irresponsible dolts!" I shout.

They scatter.

Now I come across the males—a bachelor group of five. "You should have stayed close by," I call. They look up at me, alert. "How can any of you survive when you make so many mistakes?" The billies wait to see if I'll do more than shout—to see if I'm dangerous.

The nanny cannot tell these billies what happened. She can't tell her herd. She may not even know. An eagle may be mystery to her.

But her body will understand. Her teats will swell with milk, and she'll have no one to feed. Alone. Alone, when she should have had the kid as her constant companion until this time next spring.

I'm running now, away from such senselessness.

My cave is cool and I am blinded, coming from that sunshine into this dark. I feel the floor, searching for my reed flute.

An image comes and I gasp: the eagle ripping the flesh of the kid.

I take the flute and go down to the foothills where a willow stands out from the pines, swaying in the wind. Its highest branches have already leafed out. I climb and perch up high to eat leaves. The sour green juice soaks my tongue. I hold the reed flute in both hands and play. After a half year of practice, the music eases out as though on its own.

The melody outlines the pale green of the tooth-edged willow leaves. It circles down the flaky brown bark. It creeps along the floor of the forest, past the fleshy early leaves of begonias, to a pine, then jumps from needle cluster to needle cluster. It flies from the top of the pine to the soft speckled feathers on the underside of a wood thrush that darts out of sight. It falls with the bird's droppings to the dirt that comes awake more fully each day as spring takes hold and insists. The melody enters a patch of bright yellow crocuses, making their petal cups shimmer. It gently taps the bald heads of the eaglets, who wake from their midday stupor and scream as their mother approaches. They open their mouths wide for the bits of kid entrails she drops.

I love this flute, it has given me a worthy voice. This melody plays out my world—the hard truth of a mother eagle with gaping mouths of nestlings to fill, and a mother nanny who unwittingly supplies the food. It calms me with inevitability. This is the way of my world. This is the way.

"That's you, isn't it? At last." The girl's voice is deeper than the last time I saw her, but I recognize it instantly.

"Iphigenia," I say. "Are you real or a dream?"

She smiles. Her long hair is twisted up in back. Her face has lengthened and her eyes have darkened. Her fullness swells softly under her shift, which is too thin for the weather. She points at me. "You're the one who seems a figment of the imagination. Look at you, sitting in a tree like a bird."

"Goats are found in trees now and then," I say, wondering if she'll understand the reproach in my words, the small bitterness I still hold against her.

"Did you jump up there?"

I laugh. How can she do this to me, wipe away my anger with one innocent remark? And, oh, I have to admit that there is joy in finally being part of a conversation after closing myself away all autumn and winter. "Even a goat couldn't jump from the ground to a branch this high. I climbed, my lovely."

"Then I'll climb and join you." Iphigenia lifts the front hem of her shift. She leans over and catches the back hem, pulls it forward between her legs, and ties the front and back together, exposing her legs. They are now free to move whichever way they wish.

Her ingenuity makes me laugh. But the fact that she is climbing toward me sweeps that laugh away. I am thrilled by the flexing of her thigh muscles, the smell of her hair, the wet on her lips. A young woman of her age should not climb trees, but her spirit remains pure as a child's.

I am speechless.

"I've been searching for you." She straddles the branch I'm on and shinnies her way out toward me.

"Really?" I work to keep any hint of emotion from my voice. "I'd have thought you would have forgotten about me quickly."

"No more quickly than you forgot about me."

I jerk my head back. "What makes you think I didn't forget about you?"

"You learned my name. I didn't tell you my name—I know I didn't—but you called me by it a moment ago."

Iphigenia smiles smugly. "You must have asked about me."

"I heard your mother call when I left you that day."

"Oh." Her face falls. Then she brightens. "But you remembered it."

Her voice is eager, and why should I feign indifference? "So you've been searching for me today?"

"Today and so many other days. We travel to Sparta often, and every time, going and returning, I make Mother pause for a rest at the spot where I met you. We have a name for that spot now: Lynx Land." She turns her leg so I can see the bluish scar on her calf. Her eyes go meaningfully to my left hoof.

I oblige by turning my own leg, exposing the brown scar where my knob once protruded.

"That's why I'm not allowed to go off alone anymore when we stop there. A servant always attends me." She gives me a scolding look. "I thought you weren't showing yourself because of the intrusion of my servant—but you didn't show yourself because you weren't there anymore. You changed abodes."

"The whole of nature is my abode."

"I believe that." She looks at me, those dark eyes luminous. "I heard it in your music. The music brought me to you now."

"My music didn't bring you all the way from Argos."

She laughs. "Of course not. We're traveling to Bassae,

on the west coast, and I thought I heard something, even over the noise of the horses pulling our carriage. I told Electra that if we stopped here, I'd find her perfect spring flowers. So she cried and Mother stopped." Iphigenia tucks a stray hair behind her ear. "And I found you."

"You're no less resourceful than you used to be, Iphigenia. But you've changed. You've grown."

"You've changed, too. You're different from the you that visits in my dreams."

I've visited Iphigenia in her dreams without knowing it? What part of me scrambles on a path I cannot see?

She reaches to a branch behind her head, tests it for sturdiness, then leans her head back and closes her eyes. Her skin practically glows in the sunlight. "You lied to me."

"Never."

"You said you didn't play an instrument."

"I learned since then."

She opens her eyes and shakes her head in awe. "But you play as though you were a son of Apollo himself."

My mouth fills with bile at Apollo's name. But the girl is right about my music. I have put this flute to my lips every evening since I made it. My melodies mesmerize the swans and hawks and ravens and crows—all the birds sacred to Apollo. They prefer me; every wild creature does. Mountain goats and red deer and brown bats listen, enraptured. Even the wolves of Mount Lycacus hush their howls so that they can hear.

Nevertheless, Iphigenia's praise feels good.

"Play for me."

I play the yellow doronicum petal—one of the first flowers of spring, already blessing the edge of this forest. I play the small purple bells of the wood hyacinth, which will open any day now. And the large Grecian windflowers that will bloom beneath every dogwood and flowering shrub within a moon. I play the voluptuous beauty of the pink oxalis that will follow. I play out every dizzying promise of the spring to come.

"Yes," she whispers when I stop. "I could listen to you all day and all night."

I think of playing to Iphigenia all night and my entire body tenses. "Praise can be risky."

"I like praise. My father is lavish with it."

"Ah, that father who has promised you can get married on the sands at Aulis?"

Iphigenia leans forward. "Have you learned the art of prophecy, too?" Her scent is greenest wood sorrel, tangy and fresh.

"I can read animal eyes," I say.

"Humans are not so different."

Quickly I look into her eyes. Did she really say that? Did this girl just say what I never dared hope to hear?

She smiles at me. "Can you tell me whom I'll marry?"

This is not the sort of thing eyes can tell me, in any case. Eyes tell me present thoughts—not the future. But I'm caught in the game now. I want those eyes to twinkle with glee for me. "Hold out your hand."

"Do you read fingers? Palms?" She extends her arm, fingers fanned out, straight and tense.

I take her hand and will my own not to tremble. "Let your hand go limp within mine." I stroke from the fine blue veins in her wrist, along her palm, out to her olive-stained fingertips. The surface is soft and smooth, but her hand hardly yields to mine, it is so full of anticipation. Iphigenia is easy to predict. "You'll be happy when you get news of your match."

"Get news of it? Why did you say it that way, as though it will be an announcement from a messenger?"

Why indeed? I hadn't meant to say it that way.

"Won't I be with the king and queen? Won't we discuss the youth together?"

"Apparently not." I put her hand down on the tree branch that holds her.

Iphigenia frowns. "Don't stop. Tell me about him."

"He'll be handsome," I say woodenly. After all, with her beauty, her father would never give her away to an ugly man.

"But what sort will he be? Will he be brave? And kind?"

"Brave." The word escapes me without forethought. What am I doing, pretending to know the future? But, really, saying her groom will be brave is not so different from the other things I have already said, for it follows from Iphigenia's own nature. She threw the rocks at the lynx. She returned to Lynx Land despite the reminder of danger and pain that her scar brings. She climbed this tree without a moment's hesitation. She is intrepid. Her father would never choose a weak spirit as her companion.

"What about kind? Will he be kind?"

A rotten smell invades my nose. "Why did you come looking for me?"

"You didn't answer me." Iphigenia leans toward me. "Answer. You know all about marriage."

I practically lose my balance. "What makes you say such a thing?"

She breaks off a small branch and swats my nose playfully with the leaves. "In Sparta the willow is special. Spartans make a bitter drug from the bark to fight against the ache in their bones through the damp winter. But this kind of willow is even more special. It's an *agnos castus,* the kind married women strew on their beds to keep away serpents." She blinks. "My aunt Helen in Sparta . . ." Her voice lowers with each word. "My aunt says the willow will make her fertile." She drops the branch and flushes. "Why else would you have chosen to sit in this particular kind of willow except that it is dear to you because you know about marriage?"

"I chose it because it was here, in my path."

Iphigenia scoots along the branch closer to me. She leans forward. "Are you refusing to tell me about my husband?"

The urge to lean toward her comes on me fiercely. But something's wrong. The smell grows stronger. It is the smell of fire burning flesh. "Won't your mother be missing you soon?"

Iphigenia frowns. "If you don't want to talk, I might as well go. But let's meet again."

"In a willow tree?"

"In the palace, silly. I want to introduce you to everyone."

"You don't even know my name."

"Yes, I do." That smug smile again. "I told my nursemaid about you and she said you were a satyr."

My skin crawls. "She's wrong."

"I know that. I went to the temple of Dionysus and asked the god to tell me which satyr, son of Hermes, had saved my life. He told me to fast for two days. It worked; his answer came to me in a dream. You are Pan—a unique creature. In body like the satyrs, but not in mind. Dionysus loves you."

I remember the muses fawning over me, petting me. "All the gods love me."

"As well they should," she says. "I've been looking for you partly because I never thanked you."

Partly? "I distinctly remember you thanking me," I say. I remember every word of that encounter.

"I thanked you for treating my wound. But not for fighting the lynx. For saving my life."

"You fought the lynx, too," I say.

"But it didn't matter, since you're a god and you couldn't be killed."

"You didn't know that at the time, though," I say.

"I'm thanking you, and that's that."

"It was a privilege," I say.

She smiles. "Will you come visit me soon?"

Come to the palace at Argos and see her mother, who has lied to her father about Iphigenia's birth? "What are you parents' names?"

"Queen Clytemnestra and King Agamemnon." She climbs down. "And bring your flute." She unties the knot in her shift so that it falls free again, covering those legs. Then she runs off.

She didn't even realize that I didn't agree to come to her palace, that I squirmed at the invitation. And she scurried off without gathering spring flowers. Her sister, Electra, will whine and fret.

But a moment later Iphigenia comes rushing back. "I was wrong. Apollo's sons Orpheus and Linus make exquisite music. But you don't play like them."

Must this girl always leave me with an insult?

"You play better." She blows a kiss and runs away.

I almost fall from my perch. I play better than Orpheus and Linus. Though I knew this already, Iphigenia acknowledges it. I play better than Philammon ever will—Philammon, a son of Apollo who is not yet born. Somehow in this moment I know of him. I know of a person not yet alive. Amazing. Iphigenia is right; I've changed. I know bits of the future. Knowledge comes to me.

The smell that came when Iphigenia asked me if her husband would be kind—that stench of burning flesh—returns.

Bits of the future. Her future?

I'm not in love with her. Absolutely not. I won't be Aphrodite's pawn. But Iphigenia is worthy of friendship, if any human is.

And she is worthy of protection, no matter the cost.

chapter ten

PROPHECY

The journey to Troy took more than a month. I could easily have visited Apollo's oracle at Delphi, but Apollo is the last one I want to answer my questions. There are other oracles closer to Arcadia, of course. But I don't trust them; in one way or another, each one's gift of prophecy comes from Apollo.

So I chose to travel north through Macedonia, then east across Thrace, and now south past the Hellespont into Phrygia, and, finally, to the spreading city of Troy. Cassandra lives here. Cassandra, who spins knowledge and can answer my question. Cassandra, who hates Apollo as much as I do. She can be trusted.

I must ask about Iphigenia, the girl who thinks humans and animals are not so different—the girl who looked for me all the time, only partly because she wanted to thank me—the girl who wants to know about her husband. Not will he be wealthy or handsome, but will he be brave and kind?

Mount Ida looms in the distance. The port on the coast is busy.

I see the temple of Apollo.

Once Cassandra, the daughter of King Priam, lay sleeping within that temple. Apollo came to her and whispered promises in her ear, flicking his tongue enticingly like a serpent. He offered her the art of prophecy if she would lie with him.

Knowledge for sex. To the child-woman Cassandra, the majesty of the god and the mystery of the gift must have come together like giant hands lifting her into the air, high above her fifty brothers and eleven sisters, high above her mother and father, almost as high as a god. How could she resist?

I stare at the temple. The noon sun bakes it. Spring on the Phrygian plain is hotter than in Arcadia. Poppies already rise up red and yellow—but their centers surprise with deepest black.

Red and yellow and black—like the anemones of my first meeting with Iphigenia. Everything circles back upon itself.

Cassandra is like the black center of a poppy; she surprised Apollo. Perhaps she surprised herself. For after he gave her the gift of prophecy, she refused to satisfy his lust.

A wisp of a girl tried to cheat a god. Apollo writhed in frustration: Divine favors once bestowed cannot be revoked by force. But he got the better of her. He begged for a single kiss. Cassandra loved the idea of a god pining for just one of her kisses. She parted her lips. He spit in her mouth and, thus, defiled the gift: Cassandra can tell the future better than any oracle, but that gift brings only misery, for no one believes her.

I will, though. I will listen to her and learn.

A fortress looms on the far edge of the city, built into the side of a hill. A building rises straight up from the center. Its walls arch to a point. The rear of it is lost in the hillside. And I know, I simply know, that's where I should go to find Cassandra.

I run along the inland boundary of Troy until I reach the shade of the large citadel. The stone feels cool against my hands.

"Welcome, Pan." The woman's hair falls in thick waves down her back. Her dark skin is flawless and her cheeks are high and sharp. Though she is no match for Iphigenia, she is shockingly beautiful.

"I need to ask you something."

"Don't I know that?" She leads me through the gates to the central building. She stops at the only opening, on the east side. "Soon my father will lock me in this beehive tomb."

I don't know what to say. King Priam is known for prudent governing. No one expects foul play of him.

"You doubt me." Cassandra lifts an eyebrow. "That's the curse." She takes me by both hands and dances me in circles, mirthless, pulling me so hard that I trip. She frees my hands at last. "History will say that Helen's beauty caused the bloody war between Greece and Troy—she'll be stolen away. But, in fact, the war will begin earlier—it will begin with the vengeance of my father, whose sister will soon be abducted by a Greek." She swings her hair and her eyes go wild. "Nothing ever starts where people think it does."

A war between Greece and Troy? And Iphigenia's true mother, Helen, will be named the cause? No one could steal away the Queen of Sparta. Spartans are the most ferocious warriors in the world. No one would be so foolhardy as to try.

Cassandra gives a sad laugh. "You want to know why you smell burning flesh whenever you dwell on Iphigenia's question of whether or not her husband will be kind. That's what you want, is it not?"

I nod.

"And you want to know who her husband will be. You want to know that very much."

I swallow.

"I can't tell you."

"Can't?" I ask. I feel light-headed. Gods cannot be informed of their own future. Cassandra should be able to tell me who Iphigenia's husband will be unless . . . I force the question, though it comes out as hardly more than a whisper: "Why not?"

"Cease pointless questions. The things you know yourself, Pan, they're almost like prophecy—and they serve better."

"The things I know?" I shake my head. "Scattered bits of information swirl in my mind. Hints of a messenger for Iphigenia's wedding, feelings of dread, a stench. I don't understand, though I try so hard."

"Don't try. Sometimes knowledge comes as a gift. Asclepius told you that. Accept the gift, even if it comes piecemeal. It's the best she can do."

"She?"

"The nymphs thought you were going to violate Syrinx. They turned her into reeds. But then they saw their mistake. You atone by playing that reed flute. One nymph atones with little gifts: a fact whispered in your ear, a bit of smoke blown under your nose."

One nymph. My throat catches. "My mother?"

Cassandra doesn't bother to answer. "But those gifts aren't what I meant when I spoke of the things you know yourself."

"What did you mean?"

Cassandra sighs. "Think back to Syrinx' terror. What let you feel it? Think back to what you told Iphigenia about her husband. How did you know it?"

"I thought I was pretending."

"Don't be a dunce. From the moment Syrinx told you Dryope worries about you, you changed. A drop of forgiveness entered you. You aren't just Hermes' child. You're Dryope's child, too. You've finally let that part of you speak. Listen to it." She runs to the inner wall of the citadel and climbs the stone stairs attached to the wall. "Hurry."

I'm already at her heels. From the top we see all of Troy.

She points to the temple of Apollo. "That temple houses a famous statue, the Palladium, made of dolphin bone—dolphin ivory." Cassandra looks at me out of the corner of her eye. "The dolphin is under the special protection of your newly recognized enemy, Apollo."

Enemy. My jaw closes tight. What if Apollo is listening?

"The ivory is carved in the shape of a person holding a spear aloft in the right hand, with a distaff and spindle in the left. Around the chest the aegis wraps—the beautiful breastplate with the head of a gorgon impressed on it. The soldier Aeneas will rescue it after the Greeks destroy Troy."

"The Greeks will destroy Troy?"

"Just listen. Aeneas will carry the image to Rome. People will believe that the Palladium holds the luck of Rome." She turns to me. "People believe now that it holds the luck of Troy. But it holds no luck for lost Troy."

"Why do you tell me these things?"

"Destruction lies ahead, Pan. Bloodshed, burning."

Burning flesh. "Destruction that involves Iphigenia?"

"I can't answer you."

"Do you know the answer?"

"Alas, I do."

I go down on one knee. "Help me. Please."

"You love Asclepius. I do, too. He will mourn the terrible fate of Troy. Go find Asclepius."

"Why? Asclepius' oracles don't tell the future. They tell the sick how to be healed."

"And they tell the sick how their illnesses will end."

"Iphigenia is not sick," I say. "She's not dying."

"Someone is."

"Who?"

"I can't tell you."

I stare at her. "You can't mean me. Gods don't die. You speak in riddles."

"Find Asclepius. He's reliable."

"No one is more reliable than you."

Cassandra laughs bitterly. "Is that why you have believed nothing I've prophesied so far?"

I flush in shame. "Tell me the truth and I will fight to believe you."

"You will not believe. No one can overcome Apollo's decree. But his curse does not hold of the present. So I can tell you two things. With the first, you can win what you most want to win. With the second, you can know what you most want to know."

"I'm listening." I stand tall again.

"First, contrary to your fear, Apollo is not eavesdropping now. To challenge him, the more direct approach must be employed."

"I don't want to challenge Apollo."

"It's the only way to win what you most want to win."

"What is it that I most want to win?"

"Don't be disingenuous, Pan." Cassandra descends the steps, with me right behind. "Second, remember what you already know about prophecy."

"What do I know?"

"Leave me now. Go away, Pan. I have a whole world to grieve for."

chapter eleven

TRICKERY

I am heading south along the coastal path. Soon I will turn eastward, inland to Pergamus, to find Asclepius in his sanctuary, as Cassandra bade me do.

Apollo walks in a circle, shining like the sun. Before I can skirt the path, he sees me. "Pan, my carefree fellow. What a sight for sore eyes." His smile is genuine. He doesn't realize my feelings have changed, especially toward him. "I haven't seen you since that day on Olympus—much too long ago." He comes up and claps his hands on my shoulders.

I stiffen. Cassandra talked of my challenging Apollo. Ha. I don't even have the courage to throw off his hands.

"Where have you been hiding yourself?" He pulls me to him.

I wriggle free. "Arcadia."

"Indeed? Well, no one's seen you. The muses have all been asking. What brings you to Asia Minor?"

"I'm wandering," I mumble.

"Wandering is good for the spirit. And I see you've got a flute there." He taps the reed flute that hangs from a string around my neck.

I jump backward with such violence, I fall.

Apollo laughs. "Still not a dancer. Let's hope your music is less clumsy." He helps me up. "What happened to your heel?"

I look at my knob scar. "It was that way the last time I saw you."

He shrugs. "I'm glad you're here now. You can watch the sport."

"What sport?"

"A man named Candaon hunts in the woods over there." Apollo points toward the forest to the south. "He's a skilled lover. I'm afraid that my twin sister is becoming infatuated with him."

"Artemis?" I laugh. "The goddess of maidens has nothing to do with such relationships."

"Exactly. That's her appointed role. This nonsense with Candaon has to stop." Apollo rubs his hands together. "Are you quick at finding bears, Pan?"

"Their odor gives them away."

"Good. There's a bear in those woods, undoubtedly.

Find it for me. Then I'll show you sport." Apollo takes a position behind me. "Lead the way."

"Are you hunting, as well, then?"

"Hunting, yes. The best kind. Don't delay, Pan. We haven't much time."

I don't want to help Apollo, but I haven't any excuse. And I'm not ready to displease him—if I ever will be. I go off the path into the woods. Within a few minutes I point. "Over there."

A large male bear lies asleep on his back in a clearing surrounded by oaks. Swarming insects form a black haze over his head. His muzzle must be smeared with something sweet.

"Watch my monster scare Candaon out into the sea."

Candaon? The one he's just told me Artemis loves? The plan would be cruel if it weren't so stupid. I laugh. "A brown bear isn't ferocious. It will turn tail at the first sight of a hunter."

"Ah, but it isn't a bear at all." Apollo grins. "Look again, little Pan."

Where the bear lay now lies instead an enormous scorpion. After all that has happened, Apollo couldn't have picked a creature that would bring more terror to my own heart than a scorpion.

Apollo caws loudly, like a crow.

The scorpion twists its tail, jabbing the tip down into the dirt so that it can flip itself over onto its belly. It rises on six legs. The very sight paralyzes me.

A man comes crashing through the woods into the clearing. He sees Apollo and me. He stares at the giant scorpion.

The scorpion lifts its pincers and rushes the man.

The man runs. The scorpion follows, and Apollo and I run behind.

The man is swift. When he's far enough ahead, he turns, draws his bow, and shoots. The arrow hits the scorpion's hard shell and glances aside. The scorpion keeps advancing. The man drops his bow and runs. As Apollo said he would, he jumps into the sea and swims straight out.

"Coward," says Apollo.

The scorpion stops at the shore.

Apollo flicks his hand in the air and the giant scorpion races away.

"You've had your fun. Change him back to a bear, Apollo. For pity's sake."

But Apollo is already shouting to the skies. "Artemis. Sister. Come sport with me."

Instantly, Artemis appears on the sands beside us. She hugs me with clean affection; the anger over Taugete's fawn is long gone. I hug her back, for how can I stay angry at Artemis simply because she's one of the Olympian gods?

She turns to Apollo. "What kind of sport, brother?"

"The man Candaon has just ravished Opis, one of your Hyperborean priestesses."

"My poor Opis." Artemis' eyes flash.

I watch her face; I listen to the inflections of her voice. But I hear no jealousy. Apollo must be wrong: Artemis is not the least interested in Candaon. All she cares about is her priestess.

Apollo points out to sea, to the bobbing head of Candaon on the horizon. "That's the coward there. I challenge you to shoot him."

Artemis takes an arrow from her quiver. She hits her mark.

"Well done, sister."

"I'll fetch my quarry and bring it back to Opis, so that she will know her suffering has not gone unavenged." Artemis swims out to sea.

Apollo winks at me. "Shall we go?"

For the first time since Artemis arrived, I look into Apollo's eyes, and, though I cannot know his thoughts, I see treachery. "You tricked her."

Apollo's eyes widen. "How do you know this, Pan?"

"You are known as the god of truth. So how did you do it without lying?" I search back over all that Apollo said to Artemis. Somehow she heard what he said, but she did not believe he spoke of her love. "Ah," I groan, in sad understanding, "the man Artemis cares about goes by two names."

Apollo hesitates, his mouth slightly ajar. "His other name is Orion," he says slowly.

"Yes. Yes, and Artemis had never before heard her Orion called Candaon."

Apollo steps closer. "How do you know all this?"

"Orion never ravished the priestess Opis, did he?"

Apollo shakes his head. "He's never met the maiden."

"A different Candaon violated her."

"Yes," whispers Apollo.

"How could you? How could you make your own sister kill the man she loved?"

Apollo takes me by the shoulders with a grip that hurts. "This is a new way of prophesying. Teach me this art of yours, Pan. Teach me the source of your knowledge."

All at once I understand Cassandra's words—my way of knowing is by putting myself in the other's place. Forgiveness gave me the method. "I see through your eyes."

"What can that mean?" Apollo squints. "You actually use my eyes?"

I breathe deep and take the plunge: "And what perfidious eyes they are."

Artemis' cry of misery rings out from the water.

Apollo lets go of me. "It is only because you have revealed to me the secret of your knowledge that I overlook your thoughtless remark." He is gone.

Artemis swims back, pulling the corpse. Clouds form, clouds of god tears. How can I help fight the evil Apollo has wrought? I put my reeds to my lips and play the crying of lost love. But how foolish of me. We need more than music. I run inland fast.

The sanctuary of Asclepius is at the outskirts of Pergamus, and I call to him as I approach.

"Pan? Is that you?" Asclepius runs to meet me.

"We have to hurry. Your skills must do their best."

We hug quickly and run back together.

Artemis sits on the sands with Orion's body draped across her lap. She cradles his limp head against her breasts and cries.

Two phials hang from Asclepius' neck. Both are filled with the blood of the gorgon Medusa. The master doctor opens one and taps a drop onto Orion's lips.

Orion doesn't respond.

"Try again," says Artemis.

"Two drops are forbidden."

"Then try something else. Please."

Asclepius looks at me. "Bring me the berries of an esculent oak. Hurry."

I race to the woods and break off bunches of mistletoe berries. I carry them back, running.

Asclepius has Orion on his own lap now. Artemis leans over them both, weeping. Asclepius touches Orion's chest with the berries and mutters charmed words. He touches the berries to Orion's flesh a second time. More charms. A third time.

Orion's eyelashes flutter. He lifts his head.

I whoop in joy.

Zeus' thunderbolt flashes in our midst.

Artemis screams.

My hands pull at the hair on my cheeks. Everything's turning crazy. Orion and Asclepius lie charred and blackened on the sand. I can hardly recognize their corpses.

"Father!" shouts Artemis. She runs across the sands, this way and that. Shrieks escape her with every step. "Father, don't do this to me!"

I fall to my knees, moaning over Asclepius.

But unlike Artemis, I can't cry out against Zeus. Zeus has no choice—cursèd, wicked truth. For I hear Hades, the death god of the Underworld, and the three Fates, squirreled away in the brush at the edge of the woods. Their litany is loud. They count off Capaneus, Tyndareus, Glaucus, Hippolytus. Zeus has allowed Asclepius to rob Hades of dead spirits four times already. A fifth cannot be tolerated.

I race after Artemis. I catch her around the waist and pull her to me. She beats both fists on my chest. But I hold her firm. "Hades has protested, dear dear Artemis. He won't be robbed again."

She stops moving and looks at me as though she's never seen me before.

"Accept Orion's fate," I say as gently as I can. "As I must accept Asclepius'. We have no choice. Hades has won."

"Pan." Artemis' voice is small, like a child's. Tears hang from her bottom lids. "It isn't Hades who has won. It is

Apollo. He always wins. Everything is a game to him." She rests her cheek on my chest. I feel her body give up.

Her Orion is dead.

My Asclepius is dead.

My head drops. My beard mingles with this woman's hair. The woman pressing against me is Artemis; my head tells me this. Yet her flesh yields as I imagine Iphigenia's to yield. Even in this moment of grief, the memory of Iphigenia insists. It always insists.

The odor of burnt flesh, of the flesh of Orion and Asclepius, singes my nose.

The odor of burnt flesh, which clings to Iphigenia.

I fold my arms tighter around the woman in my embrace. I become her shield.

chapter twelve

WATER

Dionysus strolls along the bank of the River Pactolus. "Look in the water, Pan. There."

The water gleams golden. "It is beautiful beyond any dream," I say.

"The four elements are mine: wine, fire, water, and gold." Dionysus smiles at me magnanimously. "Gold is my favorite." He claps his hands.

A group of maenads cluster around at the summons, dancing women draped in cloth as thin as cloud. They laugh and swirl and beg for his orders.

"Shower our Pan with gold."

The maenads disappear but return in an instant. They blow on cupped hands.

Gold dust shimmers through the air. It layers on my hairs, on my skin. I breathe the shiny metal and laugh with the women. It's been so long since I played with a maenad. I have missed them.

"At last, a bit of mirth." Dionysus links his arm through mine. "You arrived with such a scowl, I thought you might never smile again. And your smile, Pan, is the best smile in the world. Tell me why you've honored me with this visit."

"I need to be with you, good friend."

"And I am your good friend, Pan. So I know there's more to it than that."

"I need to know the future."

"Delphi is the center of the world and the finest oracle anywhere. Yet you passed it by and came all the way to Phrygia, to me?"

"Prophecy at Delphi comes from Apollo." I allow anger to creep into my voice. "I don't want Apollo's help."

Dionysus drops my arm and folds his hands behind him. He looks thoughtful.

"First I went to Cassandra, of Troy," I admit. "She sent me to Asclepius. But Asclepius just died, before my eyes."

"Then she sent you to see him die," says Dionysus.

He's right, of course. Cassandra knew what would happen. What am I to learn from such violence?

Dionysus smacks his lips. "Do you believe Asclepius is dead forever?"

"The death god Hades is the very reason Asclepius died. He won't allow the surgeon to hold back spirits anymore."

Dionysus doesn't speak.

What am I missing? And now I remember: Cassandra said that Asclepius would mourn Troy after its destruction by the Greeks. But no war between Troy and Greece has yet begun. So Asclepius must rise from the dead. It's so hard to believe Cassandra now that I've seen Hades' demands.

I've done it again: I've doubted Cassandra's predictions. I scream in frustration.

"It sounds to me as if you're in need of satisfaction, Pan." Dionysus smiles. "As in the past, as always, my maenads are yours for the taking."

I watch the women run through the woods. Satyrs scamper after them, slurping vilely. "Why do you surround yourself with satyrs?"

Dionysus laughs loudly. "Have you forgotten that life is fun?"

Whose life is fun? Surely not Syrinx' or Orion's. And what about Iphigenia? The relentless sense that she's in danger presses on me. And now I know why Cassandra wanted me present at Asclepius' death: I need to be this angry to do what I have to do. "Cassandra told me I must challenge Apollo directly to win what I most want to win."

Dionysus rubs his forehead. "Challenge him at what?"

"She didn't say."

"Ah, my dear Pan. If you've come to ask whether you'll win in a challenge against Apollo, neither of us needs to drink wine to figure that one out. Apollo will win."

"Artemis said Apollo always wins." I rub my forehead, too. It hurts horribly now. "But that's not what I came to ask. I want to know about the future husband of Iphigenia—the Princess of Argos."

"A human?" Dionysus looks at me askance. "Don't tell me you've fallen prey to the charms of a human woman."

"She's very young, barely a woman yet."

Dionysus wags a finger at me. "Not answering is the same as answering, you know. This challenge Cassandra spoke of—the one you must make to win what you most want—you didn't tell me what it is you most want to win, Pan. Tell me."

"I can't." I don't know what I want to win, I am thinking. I don't want to know.

Dionysus spreads his hands toward the waters of the river. "King Midas lives close by. He once captured my friend Silenus."

I know of Silenus. He's said to be the only wise satyr. Some say he's the father of the rest of them.

"The poor old dear wandered off and drank at a spring in which King Midas had mixed wine purposely to catch him. Nevertheless, Midas was kind to his prisoner and showed him generous hospitality. So when Midas returned Silenus to me, I granted the king a wish." Dionysus holds up one finger. "One wish." He leans toward me and hisses, "King Midas wished that everything he touched should turn to gold. The numbskull."

He laughs. "It served him right to make such a fatal wish when he had trapped Silenus in the first place. The king almost starved before he came to me imploring to be rid of the gift-curse. I had him bathe it away in the Pactolus. That's why these waters glow with the precious metal." He throws back his shoulders. "Learn from Midas, Pan. Be careful what you wish."

Everyone warns me. Everyone thinks they know my heart. I'm no fool. "Why do I smell burnt flesh when I think of Iphigenia's marriage?"

"Ah." Dionysus regards me for a while. Then he brightens. "We do need the help of wine. Let's have a celebration. For I am delighted that you've come, no matter what the reason. And it is springtime, after all." He claps again, and again we are surrounded by maenads. "Get Silenus. Call everyone together. We'll fete our guest properly."

Within minutes Silenus walks between Dionysus and me. He carries a goatskin of wine from Mount Nysa grapes. Silenus holds the goatskin out to me. "Drink, friend."

I shrink back from a container made of skin so like my own.

Silenus shrugs. Then he takes a long drink and shakes his head. "In wine lies truth; Dionysus says you seek a truth. I have a truth for you, my goat-god friend."

A maenad breaks between us and takes Silenus by one

arm. They dance ahead. The other satyrs and maenads skip around them. But Silenus is the fastest. He holds the goatskin high and squirts wine into his gaping mouth. It runs down his cheeks and chin. He laughs and dances faster. He's whirling now; his feet become a blur. His limbs lose their rigidity. They swerve, they undulate, they flow. I can no longer make out his features, he's so fast, so fluid. His paunch becomes a river, his arms the current, his hair the bulrushes.

"Silenus!" I run to the bank of the Pactolus, my arms reaching everywhere. "Silenus!"

The sigh of the wind through the reeds answers me.

"Silenus, where are you?"

Dionysus runs to me, laughing. He spins me by the elbow. "Rapture, my Pan. When emotions get too strong, Silenus cannot hold a transformation. You know how it is."

"But he just transformed."

"No, he just broke a transformation. Water is his true form. The Silenus who hugged you before is the incarnation of water. He can transform back when he calms down." Dionysus' face sparkles, as though he, too, is more water than god.

I want to talk with Silenus. He had a truth for me. The water rushes by maddeningly.

The maenads give yelps of lustful joy and the satyrs laugh raucously until the crescendo deafens me. "How can you stand this mayhem?" I shout to Dionysus.

"Who have you become, Pan? This is what it takes to break the spell of death each year—to call to life the spring. Don't you know that, you who revel in nature, don't you know?" He thrusts a bulging goatskin into my hands. "Drink, Pan. Let spring come alive in you."

Someone screams and they are all running in one direction, Dionysus, too. Frenzy captures them. I follow. They're chasing a deer, a yearling. And they're fast—as fleet as the hind. No, they are more fleet; they gain on the frantic creature. They jump on it and rip its flesh with their teeth. Within moments the animal is rent entirely; its organs splatter. Blood colors everyone's faces. Intestines dangle from their teeth.

Dionysus is on the ground with a maenad in his arms. His hands paint red on her back.

A round ball of hair rolls before me. It's from the deer's stomach, the hair this young hind licked off her friends and family. A bezoar stone.

Goats have the same thing.

I stagger away, sickened, and a savage thirst grips me. I raise the goatskin to my lips. I drink and drink until my knees wobble. I fall to the ground and close my eyes. The air is full of shouts and laughter.

Something splashes on me, but I don't open my eyes, I don't get up. The liquid seeps into my ears. It speaks. "Truth, Pan? You're seeking in the wrong place." This is the voice of Silenus. "Ask Hermes. Ask him why he's been avoiding you since you first met Iphigenia. Hear what grief a father hands to a child."

"My father is tied to Iphigenia? How?"

But the voice is silent. Inside my head a flat calm rests in empty darkness.

From this darkness comes a clear note—the cleanest, highest note my reed flute can make. Now her face appears, her deep eyes, her innocent tongue.

But it's Iphigenia's face—not Syrinx'. It's always Iphigenia. It was Iphigenia who first asked me if I could make music. It was her questions that led me to recognize the reeds as the start of my flute.

Music. That's what Iphigenia was urging me on to when she said I played better than Apollo's sons. She said it without even knowing what she was doing.

A contest of music. Me against Apollo. Of course. Apollo was always jealous of my father's music. Iphigenia told me how he bartered for Father's golden lyre, then for his reed pipe. This contest is my heritage—it is destined.

And the challenge will bring what I most want to win. But only if the contest goes in my favor.

Artemis said Apollo always wins. Always.

Everything twists back on itself.

Cassandra and Artemis can't both be right.

Artemis didn't know that Candaon was Orion. Artemis makes mistakes.

chapter thirteen

CHALLENGE

I spent the spring practicing. Nymphs gathered around me in the afternoon, and muses often joined them. They said my flute made music more beautiful than the song of any bird. They danced and laughed and cried at my melodies, as Mount Nysa echoed them. I played constantly, even in my dreams.

Today, at long last, is the contest. I am ready.

We have gathered at the palace of King Midas. Silenus suggested Midas be one of the contest judges. He bears no hard feelings toward the king for capturing him. Indeed, Silenus told me the palace food was marvelous. So Midas offered to host the affair.

I visited Apollo on Olympus to challenge him, and he didn't laugh when he accepted. At least that much he gave me.

Royalty have come from all over, troops of them. But only one matters to me: the Princess of Argos. I haven't seen her yet, but I know she is here.

Her ship sailed around the south of Argolis, past Athens, around the island of Lesbos, all the way to the coast of Phrygia. The voyage was long and the sea was rough, but Iphigenia stood on the deck, her face toward the east. The maenads told me; they seduced gulls into spying. My good friends.

And I've come to like the satyrs, too. They conceal nothing and they are ashamed of nothing. They make no apologies for being who they are.

One of the maenads tied a lynx skin around my waist. They want Iphigenia to look at me and remember that I saved her life. The maenads braid berries into the hair on my head, polish my horns to a shine with olive oil, perfume me with odors that make me woozy. They even crown me with thyme and wood sorrel, simply because I happened to mention how Iphigenia rolled in thyme the day I met her and how her breath smelled of sorrel the second time we met. They have romantic spirits, these wild women.

And maybe I do, too. For my chest swells with hope.

I never told the maenads that what I most want to win is Iphigenia's heart. They didn't need to be told. They said my heart's desire aloud, giving me the courage to acknowledge it.

Anything is possible.

Beautiful maenads lie with crude satyrs.

Anything is possible.

So here I am, staying in the damp cool of the shade thrown by a tower, while the crowds mill about. I'm not hiding, just biding my time. I hold the reed flute and wait.

The Phrygians have taken this contest as an opportunity for festivities in honor of Apollo. The morning started with a regatta on the wide Pactolus, and then the gymnasts thrilled everyone.

Now a horn blares.

It's time.

Dionysus comes in long white robes, alone. Where are my maenad and satyr friends? He slips one arm through mine and guides me to the steps of the palace.

King Midas sits in a throne at the top of the steps. A wreath of oak binds his hair behind his ears so that he won't miss a note. Pendant acorns loosely dangle to his shoulders.

The other judges sit at his sides, wearing their finest robes. The mountain god Tmolus holds the prized palm for the winner.

Spectators in lavish clothing pack the courtyard. As I scan the faces, a maenad waves to me. The satyr beside her grins. There's another pair, a way to their left. And, oh, there's a third pair. They have spread themselves out through the crowd. Every direction I look, I see friends.

Dionysus positions me on the seventh step. Then he embraces me. He pulls a small flask from the folds of his robe and offers it.

I shake my head, for this is a moment to stay sharp. I sit on my haunches.

Dionysus flows into the crowd, white overwhelmed by color. The way he merges like that makes me remember Silenus becoming river water. I want to see the old satyr's face—I have to. I stand and scan the crowd again.

There he is, nodding to me. His lips protrude and he holds his hands before his mouth as though he's blowing into a reed flute. I know he's whistling, though I can't hear it from here. Silenus thinks I'll win. He actually believes it, believes in me.

I dare to look for Iphigenia. My eyes go across the crowd. I search again, more slowly, face by face.

Apollo appears on the step beside me.

The crowd hushes.

"Are you ready, Pan?"

I can barely look at him, he lets off such dazzling light.

His purple mantle sweeps the ground. A servant makes a seat of palm leaves on the stone, and he sits and adjusts his laurel crown on his golden tresses. He looks into my eyes and puts up his hand to halt me. "No need to speak. I see the answer in your eyes. As you taught me." He laughs. "But move a step lower, goat-god. The seventh belongs to me."

The number seven is sacred to Apollo; he was born on the seventh of the month. The number four is sacred to my father; he was born in the fourth month. But no number is sacred to me. No one ever told me what day or month I was born. Maybe no one remembers. I move down a step.

The muse Polyhymnia comes up the steps carrying Apollo's lyre, and she gives me a quick, apologetic glance. The muses stopped coming to listen to me play once they found out what I was practicing for; they were caught between Apollo and me.

I look back at her with steady eyes. No one would envy the muses' predicament; no one would fault them. My eyes go to that lyre Polyhymnia carries. It's new, made of the whitest ivory inlaid with glittering jewels. The sight alone enchants. If it makes music half as lovely as its looks promise, I am lost.

Polyhymnia places the lyre in Apollo's left hand. In his right she places the long quill. The crowd gives a gasp of appreciation.

Someone coughs. And coughs. And clears her throat, her graceful throat. Across the crowd near the rear, Iphigenia smiles at me. Her father talks to the man beside him. Her mother rests both hands on a pregnant belly and whispers into the ear of Electra. They are all here—father, mother, sister. Iphigenia brought them all. She means for me to meet them at last. She waves.

I laugh out loud.

"Who first?" calls King Midas.

The question startles me. "Apollo, naturally," I say.

"You play your ditties first, Pan." Apollo smiles condescendingly. "Let the maenads and satyrs get what they deserve. Then they can leave, and I will please the worthy crowds."

The insult to my friends is worse than the insult to me.

I look to Iphigenia, to see if she has heard Apollo's brutal words, to see if she, too, despises the company I keep.

But she has left her parents' side. Where is she? Ah, I see now; she's making her way through the crowds to the front. Her eyes are on me. In the months since we last met, she has become an utterly glorious woman. Her parents must already talk to her about her marriage.

But her face reminds me I must keep my mind on the moment. I must win the right to touch that face.

I put one hand above my brow as a shield from Apollo's brightness, and I look at his stern face now. Someone has reported to Apollo on my playing—I can feel his anxiety. Perhaps he even came in disguise as a badger or a wild boar to listen to me in the evenings. Now he's hoping that I've become more like the companions of Dionysus; that's why he insulted them. He wants me to give in to my impulses and walk away in a huff, conceding the contest to him. Apollo actually fears I may win this contest.

"As you wish," I say. I stand and bow to the crowd. "Thank you for coming, good friends."

Scattered applause rises from every direction. Faithful maenads, faithful satyrs. I smile my gratitude.

Then I play. The sound comes stiff at first, as though my lungs are asleep. But gradually the music wakes and stretches. I play the shortening of late-summer days, how the south wind, Notus, leaves the white trumpet flowers swinging, how the foxes' fur thickens. I move on, day by day, week by week. I play the hardwood trees, shocked at the first frost, changing the color of their leaves to seductive hues of yellow and red, and the north wind, Boreas, blowing off those leaves once they've shriveled to brown, and the hares lining their burrows with the fallen leaves. I play the early-winter stars in the night sky—the hapless Orion followed continually by the giant scorpion, both thrust into the heavens by Artemis in her sorrow—and the snow clouds that will obscure stars and moon in the month that follows. I play the silent wonder of goats in the long lonely mystery of winter.

As I play I watch the faces of the crowd, how their cheeks go from red to almost blue, how they shiver. Iphigenia wraps her arms around herself as though trying to hold in her own heat. Her eyes plead.

My reed flute relents, just as nature must. The east wind, Eurus, comes off the Aegean Sea, across the plains, carrying warm wetness to the waiting earth. I play the stirring of the roots within the soil, the rainbow colors of the early-spring flowers, the buzz of bees, the whir of hummingbird wings, the willowy spring of newborn hedgehogs' spines.

Iphigenia smiles.

Courage comes to me. I play Zephyrus, the sweetest and mildest of the winds, caressing Iphigenia's cheeks; delicate rambling roses brushing her nose; a finger, godlike, kissing her lips as lightly as a memory. I play all her hopes of a brave husband, a husband who would dare to challenge a god to win her. I play all her hopes of a kind husband, a husband who would respond to all her desires, who would give anything to keep her safe. I play without time or space, in a magic I've never known, a magic I have longed for since I met her.

I finish, exhausted.

The crowd cheers. Iphigenia jumps in place, clapping and laughing.

"Well, done, Pan." Apollo's voice comes from behind me, deep and low, so that only I can hear. It is a strong voice. If he is worried, he gives no hint. "Your crude rural melodies have pleased many. But even the vulgar throng can recognize refinement. Listen, and learn."

I sit and look up at him.

He raises the quill, gives a meaningful look to the judges on the steps above us, and begins.

With the first vibrations of the lyre strings, the crowd goes silent. The lyre commands reverence.

I know Apollo's thoughts, Apollo's intentions, so I know what this lyre plays, anticipating a half second before each note. It plays the radiance of the divinities: Zeus with his thunderbolts and Poseidon with his trident; Athena springing from Zeus' forehead and Aphrodite coming alive in Poseidon's sea foam; Hades in his Underworld and Artemis in the forests; Hestia, the goddess of the hearth, and Hephaestus, who used the hearth for forging; Ares, the god of war, and Hera, the goddess who railed against her philandering husband; and, finally, my solemn father, Hermes, who guides the souls of the dead to their final home, and Apollo himself, who guides us all to the joy of sunshine each day.

I want to object to this last contrast. Hermes does so much more than guide the dead. It was Hermes himself who taught Apollo to play the lyre. Why isn't Hermes here to defend himself?

Why isn't he here to cheer on his son?

Has he really been avoiding me?

But Silenus was surely wrong when he said this inside my head, for it is I who have refused to see Hermes for ever so long, I who have steadfastly avoided the Olympian gods.

The moment to protest passes. The lyre's music now celebrates the splendors of Apollo: how he first taught man the art of healing; how no false word ever falls from his lips; how valuable are his many oracles, especially the one at Delphi; how he has taught the art of prophecy to every reputable seer.

And, again, I am bursting with the need to correct him.

Apollo has no right to boast of his healing art after he caused the death of the finest physician the world has ever known. And he robs the word *truth* of meaning, given how he tricked Artemis into shooting Orion. But most of all his claim about teaching prophecy to all seers is a lie. He never taught me. Rather, I'm the one who taught him to see through others' eyes. I taught him. Me.

But the lyre plays on. It plays the way Apollo can shoot an arrow farther than anyone. It plays his beautiful countenance, his perfect body, his soft rich hair.

I have no defense.

The crowd cheers longer and more loudly than they did for me.

"The winner is"—King Midas pauses for effect—"Pan."

"What? You idiot! The crowd has chosen me." Apollo marches up the steps. He knocks the oak wreath from Midas' head and pulls on the king's ears. "Ass ears. That's what you have."

Instantly, donkey ears replace Midas' own—long gray donkey ears. The stunned king's mouth hangs open.

"You're lucky I don't give you a bray."

"You're absolutely right, Apollo. You are the winner." Tmolus hands the winner's palm to Apollo.

Apollo holds it high.

The crowd shouts the righteousness of this decision.

I run down the steps. But in my terrible haste, I stumble and roll to the bottom. I get to my hooves and race away from the laughter. Away from people who value the riches of the mighty over the riches of the earth. Away from thc woman Iphigenia, who has seen me fail so extravagantly.

I hear the calls of the maenads and the satyrs, shouting behind me, crying out the injustice of the contest, loyal to the end. It is as though I've become Dionysus, with a train of followers.

But I want no followers.

I want no one.

chapter fourteen

DECEPTION

"Stop!" Father's voice is unmistakable, but I keep running.

Father blocks my path.

I smack into him, and we fall. His arms hold me fast. We wrestle.

"It's over, Pan."

I give up the struggle, for he is the god of gymnastic skill. My body goes limp.

"You should have won," he says.

"I didn't see you in the crowd."

Hermes sits. "The muses told me about it."

So I was right. "Funny how you didn't listen for yourself." I roll on my side so that my back is to him.

"You didn't want me there."

"How do you know?"

"Cassandra told me."

"No one believes Cassandra," I say.

"No one believes her about the future. But I talked to her as the contest began."

I get into a squat. "Apollo has an ivory lyre now. Did you know that? He doesn't even use the golden one he tricked you out of."

Father touches the scar at the back of my left ankle. I move away quickly. He gives a sad noise, almost like a whimper. "Apollo can play on a lyre made of jewels. It doesn't matter. You'll always make more enchanting music than he does."

I stand. "How would you know?"

"I listen to you every night. You play the sweetest pipes I've ever heard."

Father has been hovering close by and I didn't know? "Why would you listen?"

"I love you."

I wince and circle him. "You've been avoiding me," I say to his back.

Father's shoulders twitch.

Silenus was right. I stand in front of him. "Ever since I met Iphigenia, you've been avoiding me."

Father stares at his feet—at those chiseled, winged, perfect feet. Nothing like my hooves.

I put my hands on his cheeks and tilt his head upward. Gloom and disaster fill his eyes. My guts twist. "What? What have you come to tell me?"

"This love isn't worth it."

"Worth what?"

"What does the love of a human woman amount to anyway?" he says. "The flicker of a candle. Humans barely live."

He said something like this, something very like this, the morning of the day I first met Iphigenia. Was he trying to warn me off loving her even then? How much did he know in advance? What does he conceal?

Father is known as the god of trickery. Of deceit. But I never before thought he would deceive me.

He is Apollo's brother.

"Cassandra was right," I say, "I didn't want to see you."

"Don't be like this, Pan. It's over. Come with me, come be my merry boy again, the one who makes us laugh. Come before you seal your fate. Be with those you belong to for all eternity. Get away from that disgusting throng of satyrs."

Satyrs never deceive. "Good-bye, Father."

part three

LETTING GO

chapter fifteen

SMEARED MEMORIES

Rolling in high grasses. Grainy smells in my nose. Hands tugging, kneading. Kisses. Some maenad or other.

Sharp bursts of pleasure.

I laugh till I gag.

Racing over the foothills, slaying any wild beast that crosses the path. Blood, like wine, like water. Not knowing—not caring—whose.

Shaggy, watching the moon goddess Selene. Knowing her secrets. Her face round, naively greedy for a beautiful white fleece I am only too happy to deliver. Promises spilled on the earth. Into the Arcadian woods. Me, tricky as my uncle. As my father.

The clash of cymbals. The shrill of pipes and waving, burning brands. Ecstatic maenads. Everything moving, swirling, trees and rocks and sky. Blissful oblivion.

Nymphs. Echo and Pitys. Chasing like animals. A shower of blood. A pine tree. Someone escapes. But there are always others; always ways to despoil the lesson of Syrinx.

A loutish Pan, whose violations are too many to hold in memory. A Pan who never suffers from too much thought.

Then crying. For once it isn't me. For once I am sober enough to know that for sure.

A boy. He introduces himself as Daphnis, my half brother. That scoundrel Hermes has fathered so many, the world is populated with my half brothers. I don't question the source of this boy's misery—I understand. We share a little wine and I teach him to play on my reed flute. He smiles and learns fast.

One peaceful day.

More crying. This time it's a girl, a human, with a broken heart. It is early enough in the day, early enough in my drinking, that I can hear her whisper: She calls herself Psyche. She wants to die for failed love. All I can offer are words, melodic words. Comfort. She marvels that I understand her pain so well. She asks, "Have you been unlucky in love?" I tell her, "Not unlucky, cursed." She stops crying and croons to me. It almost feels good. But when she leaves, the numbness returns. The air shimmers.

I reach for the wineskin.

chapter sixteen

ABDUCTION

I lie on the ground and look up at a god who claims to be my father. If he only knew what I've become, he'd never be here.

But of course he would. He recognizes himself in me—and he cannot reject himself.

I am just like him. No—what did Syrinx say? I've surpassed Hermes—I'm just like Apollo. We're all randy as goats.

The curse of Aphrodite.

The loss of Iphigenia.

And why am I thinking so clearly? Where's my wineskin? My fingers search the floor of the cave.

Hermes' hand reaches out at the same moment.

"Don't." I retract. "Don't pet me. Ever."

"No one would think of petting you. You're filthy. You

stink. I was merely going to pick a ball of matted hair from your leg."

"What? You don't find me as beautiful as Apollo?" I laugh so hard, I break into coughs. I feel a tug on my leg. It hurts.

Hermes holds an ivory comb. He takes hold of my right ankle and pulls my leg straight. He combs roughly.

I try to yank my leg back under me, but he holds firm. I yank again, though it's obviously futile. "I've never been good at wrestling. This is one way, at least, that I don't follow in your footsteps." I laugh. "Hoof steps, rather. Not footsteps."

"Stop pitying yourself."

"You should have hooves. Like me. You're bestial, too."

Hermes shakes his head. "Despite your drunkenness, you still play the sweetest pipes."

I look around. There's my wineskin. I lunge.

Hermes kicks it out of reach.

"What right do you have to deny me?" I shout, "Dionysus, friend, where are you?"

"You need to be sober now, Pan."

"Dionysus!" I shout again. "Help me."

"He's gone." Hermes combs my leg hair so hard, it brings tears to my eyes. "He wouldn't come to your aid now anyway. We're in this together."

"In what together?" I grip his wrist with both my hands. "What conspiracy do you speak of? Who is this 'we'?"

"All of us, all who love you."

"No one loves me."

Hermes snorts. "The Greek people adore you."

"Adoration isn't love."

"What about your half brother Daphnis? This past winter when he came to you lonely, you taught him to play the pipes. He reveres you."

"Reverence," I practically growl. The word tastes rotten in my mouth. "That's not the same."

"And what about Psyche? You comforted that poor girl after she attempted suicide. You counseled her to open her heart to Eros."

"Gratitude!" I shout. "Don't you know anything? Don't you have any idea of what love is?"

"The maenads love you."

"The maenads roll in the grass with anyone who will have them." My disloyal words shock me, even in the state I'm in. I hope the maenads have not heard; I hope I have not hurt my true friends.

Hermes lets go of my right leg and grabs the left. He combs again. "Let's get you clean. Then you can transform fully into a god."

"What kind of shabby trick is this? I can never be whole—never completely goat, never completely god."

Hermes combs my entire leg, whistling the while. When he's finished, he lets go.

I stand immediately. "What are you doing here?"

Hermes looks at me hard. "You resemble me, you know—in your face and in your ways. But you're better skilled at the flute and the art of prophecy."

My head hurts and my mouth feels as if small animals have been nesting in it. "Your sincerity is overdue. It's dead."

Hermes gathers pebbles within reach and casts them from his right hand.

"Are you divining?" I ask. "What part of the future do you want to know?"

Hermes looks up from the pebbles. "There's another part to the curse. A part I never told you. A part I hoped you'd never face."

Trembles come. I grit my teeth against them.

"Your love of nature made Artemis care for you so much that she added a provision to the curse."

"What provision?"

"You can never transform into goat or god unless you love someone truly and she loves you back. Then you can transform one last time—you can be whole."

Whole.

"Love?" I say as lightly as I can. "Why would you have hoped I'd never face this?"

"Love is painful."

Brash in my ears comes Apollo's noise from that day with the muses: Human love is suffering. An intensity that cannot withstand eternity. A joke. How like the brothers to agree. I give a small laugh. "You understand nothing of love, Father. If a woman truly loved me, there would be no need to transform. She wouldn't care if I were half goat."

Father doesn't speak.

"Why have you chosen to tell me all this now?"

"Because of Iphigenia."

The sound of her name smothers me. No one has dared utter it near me since the day of the music contest.

I walk outside the cave for air and immediately hunch over. My hands shield my eyes from the blinding sun. My stomach clenches.

Hermes' hand comes heavy on my shoulder. "A Trojan named Paris abducted the Spartan queen Helen."

Cassandra was right again. Against all odds, Iphigenia's mother has been stolen away to Troy. I remember Theseus. "That's the second time Helen has been taken against her will."

"Not against her will this time. Paris seduced her by playing the flute."

Seduced by a flute? Would that the daughter had the weakness of the mother. But no. I never set out to seduce Iphigenia. I set out to win her heart.

"This Paris turns out to be a banished prince of Troy. So the violation involves the royalty of both nations. The Greeks have armed many ships. They will set sail for Troy to bring Helen back—and a ten-year war will start. All of it will start as soon as the winds blow at Aulis."

"What has this to do with me?"

"That's up to you. But it has much to do with Iphigenia."

Inside my head thunder rolls, the herald of Zeus, telling me to listen well. Nothing good can happen now. "How?"

"Her father, King Agamemnon, gathered troops at Aulis. While they were still stocking the ships, the king went hunting. He killed a fine stag with a single arrow and boasted that he was a better hunter than Artemis herself."

"The fool."

"Artemis in her outrage bid all the winds to stay home. The Greek fleet cannot sail until Agamemnon makes a suitable sacrifice."

Blood again. "Go on," I whisper.

"Artemis has demanded that Agamemnon sacrifice his fairest daughter."

"An ungodly demand." My voice becomes a screech. "Artemis protects maidens, she doesn't kill them." But even as I speak, I remember Artemis' anger when the lynx killed Taugete's fawn. She couldn't still hold a grudge against Iphigenia, could she? Could she close such a terrible circle? "Anyway," I say in desperation, "Iphigenia isn't Agamemnon's daughter. She is the child of Helen and Theseus."

"Agamemnon doesn't know that."

"He needs to be told. When is this sacrifice to take place?"

"Tomorrow. But transform first, Pan. You love her; she loves you. You can do it now. Go to the king as a god—all god."

I sling my reed flute around my neck.

"Transform!" shouts Father as I race away. "Transform."

chapter seventeen

SACRIFICE

Iphigenia stands in the moonlight at her window. She seems as defenseless as the newborn kid before the eagle.

I walk across the courtyard straight to her.

She focuses on me with difficulty. "Is that you, Pan?"

"Perhaps I should play a song?"

The corners of her mouth lift the tiniest bit. "With or without your flute, I know you, dearest friend. I have danced to your words, not just your music, for years; dreams can be good that way."

"Why are you here in Aulis?" I ask.

"My father sent for me." Her eyes widen in sudden realization. "Just as you said, he sent word—an announcement. And I was happy. Just as you said. But when I got here, he told me I would marry the brave warrior Achilles."

"He deceived you, Iphigenia. He brought you here falsely."

"I know. Tomorrow I die."

"No." I climb over the windowsill into the room and take Iphigenia's hands. "Artemis has not demanded you. She demanded your father's fairest daughter."

"Father chose me."

"Because he doesn't know you're not his own."

"He loves me. He must never know that I'm not his." Iphigenia shakes her head slowly. "Never."

"Nonsense. He'd want to know, Iphigenia. If he truly loves you, he'd never want you killed. I'll tell him myself."

"No, you won't. You keep my secrets. I trust you, Pan. I trust you more than anyone."

"To be worthy of that trust, I must tell your father."

Iphigenia pulls her hands from mine and puts them on my cheeks. She smoothes my tufts and cups my face. "Dear Pan. Don't you understand? If I don't die, Electra dies." Her eyes are glassy with tears.

"I can argue with Agamemnon. If he sacrifices no one, then the ships cannot sail and the carnage of war will never take place."

"This war must take place." Iphigenia's hands fold over my ears, run to the tips of my horns. "Without the war, Helen, my true mother, cannot be brought home, her shame cannot be ended."

She has rallied too many arguments. I feel myself slipping. "Who told you Helen was your true mother?"

"Queen Clytemnestra, of course. A mother tries to save her own children, after all." Iphigenia gives a sad little laugh. "And to think I always wanted to know who my true mother was."

"Clytemnestra was brutal to tell you."

"She cries for me, Pan. Almost as much as she would have cried for Electra or my baby brother, Orestes. Pity her."

"I can't let you do this."

"Achilles wants to stop me, too. He came and talked with me. For a warrior, he is too gentle."

My eyes sting. I have to bite the inside of my cheeks to keep from denouncing the man.

"But neither of you can stop me," says Iphigenia. "I won't let you." She kisses my forehead. A kiss, at last.

"Iphigenia," I murmur, wishing I wouldn't—it feels obscene in this moment—knowing I must. "You said you were happy when you got the announcement that you would marry. Then you said, 'But when I got here, he told me I would marry Achilles.' " I swallow. "You said, 'The brave warrior Achilles.' Why did you say 'but'?" My voice becomes a whisper. "Were you no longer happy?"

"I was confused."

"Why?" I breathe.

"You needed me. I sensed that before, but the day of the contest I understood, even though you ran from me. Whom does Achilles need? No one."

"Need is a far cry from love," I dare to say.

"How so? Love is so many things. Need. Hope. All that brought you here tonight." She shakes her head slowly. "There's no point to this conversation, dear one. Everything has changed.

"I'm very tired, but I haven't been able to sleep for the past two days. Since I found out. I fought, I pleaded, I plotted my escape. But in the end, I realized there is no other way. All I want now is to sleep. Play for me, Pan. Play as you play in my dreams. You are the best musician. You told me once that you're a minor god. But you're the greatest of gods, for you are nature itself." She walks to her couch and curls on her side. "Your song and your song alone can bring me peace. Play," she whispers.

"Iphigenia . . ." My voice barely comes.

"No other way," she whispers.

No other way.

But one.

My fingers slip on the reeds, everything wet with tears.

chapter eighteen

LOVE

Iphigenia climbs the hill at the edge of Artemis' meadow. Hyacinths cover her head, woven into her curls.

The priest-executioner waits at the top. He holds his sword at the ready. A black hood covers his head.

The crowds stay at the foot of the hill and watch the smoke rise from the sacrificial fire.

Artemis stands in the woods beside me. She's been still as dead water for many minutes, but now she trembles. "No. I can't be part of this."

"You have to. You agreed."

"Only because I owe you, for fetching Asclepius to save Orion. But the payment is out of balance. It's wrong—it makes no sense. No!"

"You can't back out now."

"Yes, I can." Her eyes rage. "She's human, Pan. She'll die soon anyway."

"Soon to you, not to her. To Iphigenia a human lifetime is long."

"Immortality is longer." Artemis' voice breaks. "No other god has ever given it up. No one. Don't throw it away lightly, Pan."

Nothing is light for me. The very air sleeps leaden on my shoulders.

She's crying now. "Don't, Pan. I can't bear it. You know how I love you."

"And I love you, dear aunt. That's why you must help me. I can't do it without you." I wipe the tears from her cheeks and straighten her shoulders. She sighs in resignation. "Tell me you will make the announcement, as you promised," I say.

"I have already chosen the sailor, one Thamus, who will shout it to the universe."

"And he will use the word *great*? He will call out, 'The great god Pan'?"

"Yes, and everyone will cry. All humans, all gods."

I don't care whether or not everyone cries. I care only about Iphigenia. "And you will take care of her?"

"She will be safe with me in Thrace. And her mother, Helen, will be saved at the end of this war. Helen will dedicate a temple at Argos to Eileithyia, the birth goddess, in love of Iphigenia, and she will decorate it with stags, in gratitude to me." She swallows a sob. "If you must do this terrible thing, yes, everything you want will happen."

Everything I want.

This is what I have negotiated.

I could have swept Iphigenia away to live with me somewhere safe.

But I never could have stopped her tears over Electra's death.

So maybe I'd have lost her love anyway.

"It's time," I say. "The sword grows heavy in the executioner's fist." I hand Artemis my reed flute. "This is my voice. Give it to Silenus, please."

Artemis takes the flute.

"Don't transform!" Hermes stands in my way.

"The last time I saw you, you felt differently. You contradict yourself, Father."

"If you had become a whole god when I told you to, you'd never be able to do this stupid thing now. I tried to stop you. Why didn't you listen?"

It's funny how I thought then that the ability to transform fully into god or goat wouldn't matter if Iphigenia loved me truly. Oh, it matters. It matters. And the glory is that ordinary goat—not god—will bring the end I need.

"If you had only transformed then," says Father, "Iphigenia would have loved you properly."

Properly. Father has so little idea of what that means. "Even if she loved me till she died, I would have spent the rest of eternity mourning her."

"As I will mourn you." His face crumples with grief.

I kiss Father on both cheeks. Then I put my hands to the godly flesh on my naked chest and touch for the final time.

I transform into goat. Whole, at last.

My goat body cannot stay still. It springs on four legs. I leap up the other side of the hill to meet Iphigenia just steps from the executioner.

She lets out a little burst of air. "Shoo, poor creature. Run for your life."

I come to her feet and press against her legs.

She touches my ear tenderly, then lets her hand run lightly down my neck, along my back, down my leg. "Ahi! This hoof is missing a knob."

Artemis takes Iphigenia by the arm. "It's time to go." She jerks her chin toward Hermes. "Loan her your winged slippers, brother. Do our Pan this final favor."

Iphigenia looks from me to Artemis and Hermes, then to me again. "No! I won't let you do this." Her cry is a knife to any other heart, but to mine it comes as balm. "My dearest Pan." She is sobbing. "No."

But the executioner holds his sword aloft.

My love is whisked away.

The sword flashes, dazzles, as it falls.

Afterword

Classical myths have many variations from one telling to another. The stories of Pan and Iphigenia, for example, present a range of possible parents for each of them. But all versions of their stories leave two gaps.

In Plutarch's *Moralia,* the sailor Thamus calls out, "The great god Pan is dead." Pan is the only god who is ever reported to have died. There is no explanation for this claim, and Greek scholars have debated whether the interpretation of those lines is correct.

On Iphigenia's side, there are many accounts of why King Agamemnon decides to sacrifice her. But all those I read agreed that when the executioner had dealt the fatal blow, a hooved animal lay sacrificed on the ground rather than the maiden. Again, there is no explanation. Iphigenia next shows up as a priestess in Artemis' Tauric temple in Thrace. After her "death," the wind blows, allowing the Greeks to set sail for Troy and begin the ten-year war that Cassandra foretold to Pan, ending in the destruction of Troy and the return of Helen to her husband, King Menelaus of Sparta.

With this book I have tried to fill both gaps.

about the author

DONNA JO NAPOLI is the author of many distinguished books for young readers, among them *Daughter of Venice, Crazy Jack, The Magic Circle, Zel, Sirena,* and *Stones in Water.* She has a B.A. in mathematics and a Ph.D. in Romance linguistics from Harvard University and has taught widely at major universities in America and abroad. She lives with her family in Swarthmore, Pennsylvania, where she is professor of linguistics at Swarthmore College.